GLIPTON ROMEOS

'Girls will always be around. . . . Football is a delicate bloom.'

At the start of the new season, Jossy Blair, team manager of the Glipton Giants, had never bargained for his lads going soft over a bunch of girls – and it takes a few underhand tactics to persuade them back to the turf. When he does though, even Jossy finds a touch of romance in his soul.

'Sid Waddell's book is tight, well written and, most important, alive. . . . Waddell knows his football and it shows.'

Children's Books (Of Sid Waddell's first book *Jossy's Giants*)

This book is based on the second BBC TV series featuring Jossy and his team – *Jossy's Giants II* by Sid Waddell, produced by Paul Stone and directed by Edward Pugh. The main characters were played as follows: Jossy, Jim Barclay; Glenda, Jenny McCracken; Ross, Mark Gillard; Tracey, Julie Foy; Glenn, Stuart McGuiness; Selly, Ian Sheppard; Melanie, Lucy Keightley; Harvey, Julian Walsh; Opal, Suzanne Hall; Ricky, Paul Kirkbright; Shaz, Jenny Luckraft.

About the Author
Sid Waddell is a Geordie, born in a pit village eighteen miles north of Newcastle-upon-Tyne. There football was a part of life: the boys played all day and half of the night – and the ambition of every one of them was to play for Newcastle United.

Sid's career has been in television and he is known to millions as a BBC darts commentator. Married with five children, Sid Waddell lives in Yorkshire.

The idea for the two books starring the Glipton Giants came when Sid's son Daniel started to play for Churwell Lions, a boys' team in West Leeds.

GLIPTON ROMEOS

Sid Waddell

BBC/KNIGHT BOOKS

To
Boss Rene
and the rest of
the South Parade Mafia

Copyright © Sid Waddell 1987

*First published 1987 by the British Broadcasting Corporation/
Knight Books*

British Library Cataloguing in Publication Data

Waddell, Sid
    Glipton romeos.
    I. Title
    823'.914[J]   PZ7

    ISBN 0-340-40913-4
        (0-563-20564-4) BBC

Printed and bound in Great Britain for the British
Broadcasting Corporation, 35 Marylebone High Street,
London W1M 4AA and Hodder and Stoughton
Paperbacks, a division of Hodder and Stoughton Ltd.,
Mill Road, Dunton Green, Sevenoaks, Kent (Editorial
Office: 47 Bedford Square, London WC1B 3DP) by
Richard Clay Ltd., Bungay, Suffolk. Photoset by
Rowland Phototypesetting Ltd., Bury St Edmunds, Suffolk.

ONE

Jossy Blair swaggered out of St James's Park, Newcastle-upon-Tyne, feeling as if he had, in football jargon, 'done great'. He plonked a large, plastic-rope sack of footballs on the pavement and breathed in deep lungfuls of pure air straight off the river. Life was ace; his scrounging trip to United's ground had paid off, he had made his twice yearly pilgrimage to his home village of East Slackburn and now, before returning home to Glipton, he was on his way for a pint at The Magpie's Nest with an old friend – the legendary Johnnie the Runner.

Head high, Jossy bounded along Sandgate and down a cobbled alley in the shadow of the proud arches of the Tyne Bridge. The Magpie's Nest was certainly not what you could call a 'fun pub'. It was more the kind of spot Fagin and the Artful Dodger would have used for 'business meetings'. Alongside the modern lighting were old gas mantles, preserved inside smoky glass holders. United heroes like Hughie Gallacher and Jackie Milburn beamed down on the punters from browning photographs. Johnnie the Runner looked as though he had been sitting on his stool by the bar since the original Blaydon Races in 1862.

Johnnie's eyes lit up when Jossy entered the bar. He adjusted his battered old trilby hat and shot the cuffs of his shirt. A frill of old racing tickets hung in the lapel of his jacket like a good-luck charm. He called in the pints.

'What cheer, bonny lad?' The darting eyes latched on to the footballs Jossy was carrying. 'By, your business down in Manchester must be booming if you've come all this way on a sales trip.'

'Chance would be a fine thing,' replied Jossy, nuzzling into the beer. 'I cadged these balls from St James's Park for my lads' team, the Giants.'

'Are they good?' asked Johnnie.

'Triers, in the main. But when the spirit moves them, they can't half turn it on a bit.' Jossy cast a casual glance at the crumpled issue of *The Sporting Life* on the bar top.

Something flared in Johnnie's eyes. He picked up the paper. 'There's a real cracker of a horse running in the half-past three at Redcar today. Galloway Gourmet. Worth a fiver each way.'

Jossy could not return the avid grin. He fixed his gaze on a poster advertising *Doxford's Dog Food Domino Handicap*.

'Changed your spots, have you, kidda?' Johnnie tapped the paper. 'I remember the time you'd have been off down the bookie's like a ferret down a hole.'

Jossy's lean face twitched with something very like embarrassment.

'I've been laying off the gee-gees recently, old son. I got into a bit of bother.'

Johnnie's eyes narrowed and he gave Jossy the once-over.

'You're looking a bit smarter than I remember. Could it be that there's a lady in your life?'

Jossy blushed and began to bluster. 'Hang on, kidda, you know me better than that.'

The old man supped off his pint.

'Do you good to settle down. I'll buy the next drink. Save your money for your sweetheart.'

It was not worth Jossy arguing. There had always

6

been something of the fortune-teller about Johnnie Sinclair. And Galloway Gourmet would probably be a sure thing . . .

He resisted the temptation. Glenda Fletcher and he had stepped out socially together a couple of times recently – unknown, of course, to the Giants. The bingo at Glipton Workingmen's Club had not seemed to impress Glenda; and the work of somebody called Boulez by the Hallé band had left Jossy absolutely cold. But one thing seemed to be understood between them – Jossy's betting days were over.

Johnnie launched into a story about a great day out at York Races. Jossy listened but kept one eye on the clock. The Giants, Albert Hanson and Tracey Gaunt would all be at Glipton Station eager to meet the 3.15 arrival from Newcastle.

The dream images of Jossy's train-lulled sleep were very garbled. They were a mixture of the realities of the Glipton Giants' exploits the previous season and wild fantasies of Jossy's imagination. The pitch was apparently on the Tyne Bridge, high above Newcastle. Ricky Sweet was leading the Giants in a 5-a-side against their arch-rivals, the Ecclestone Express. A tall, severe man with a dark moustache and dressed like a civil servant sneered at Jossy. It was Dave Sharkey, manager of the Express. Pulsing with fiendish strength, he picked up Jossy and hurled him down into the grey waters of the Tyne. Jossy splashed and began sinking. Then a boat appeared, rowed by Glenda Fletcher, dressed like a milkmaid, and singing:

'I canna get to my love if I would dee,
  For the waters of the Tyne run between
    him and me.'

7

Jossy reached out for the oar. But something like giant hailstones began bombarding him . . .

Jossy awoke with a start to find the bag of footballs in his lap. He began to wrestle with them – then stopped when he realized people in the carriage were staring at him. The train was really tearing along on the fast stretch near Thirsk. He replaced the balls on the luggage rack and pretended to go back to sleep.

Albert Hanson fiddled with the knot of his tie. Trying to look smart in a business suit with all the trimmings was still new to him. But since he and Jossy had become partners in Magpie Sports, as well as in the management of the Giants, Albert was determined to make a go of looking the part. He sipped a cup of Bovril in the buffet of Glipton railway station and prayed that Jossy would be in a good mood. Albert had tried – oh, how he had tried – to raise even the shadow of a reception committee. But to no avail . . .

'The next train to arrive at Platform Two will be the 3.15 arrival from Newcastle . . .' The metallic, bingo-caller tone of the announcer echoed round the buffet. Albert shot to attention. He walked casually on to the platform as the yellow nose of the train slithered towards him.

'Hey up, kidda!' Jossy was off the train and running almost before it had stopped. He bear-hugged Albert and then his lean features crinkled with bleak surprise.

'The lads hiding in the left luggage, are they? Ready to give me a surprise, eh?' Jossy looked about. 'Come out, come out, wherever you are!'

Albert could not look him in the face.

'Don't tell me that Dave Sharkey has pirated the lads for the Express. I'll report him to the league and the FA.'

Albert focused his gaze on a mill chimney two miles over the valley.

'There's been a marked lack of keenness for the start of the new season, Jossy. I've spread the word about a training session tomorrow, but . . .'

Jossy's eyes narrowed.

'But?'

'But – they all say they're too busy!'

Jossy crashed the bag of footballs down on the platform. He stuck his neck out like an angry rooster.

'Busy! That's gratitude for you. I've run my legs off all over Geordieland for the past two weeks cadging gear. I've pattered and pleaded for everything from footballs to embrocation. And what do I get for my efforts? A one-man reception committee!'

Before Albert could further the discussion, a minor drama taking place at one of the train doors caught their attention. It featured a lad of about seventeen, with short-cropped hair, who was hanging half-out of the window, clutching a fair-haired girl with her back to Jossy and Albert. As the whistle blew for the train to depart, the lad's voice echoed down the platform.

'I can't go. I can't do it. I need you every living moment.' The lad was giving it the full Paliachi. Jossy and Albert crept nearer, ear-wigging.

The girl broke the half-nelson the lad had on her neck. She tossed her head and spoke like a staff nurse.

'Don't be daft, Rupert. It was only a holiday romance. I'll see you at the Hockey International.'

More passionate blood filled the lad's face as the train began to move. 'Write, do write, dearest Tracey.'

Tracey Gaunt waved a casual hand and turned. She got a shock to see Albert and Jossy. The look on Jossy's face was very peevish. The lips pulled back from the teeth. The voice trembled with hurt. 'I never thought I'd see the day. Tracey Gaunt going loopy over a lad – and in a public place!'

The face stayed calm; the blue eyes icy. 'You should

know me better than that, Jossy Blair. I'm not the kind to go loopy over lads or owt else.'

Jossy did not seem convinced. He pointed at the rapidly disappearing train and the lad who was still waving frantically.

'You'll have plenty of time for fellas in later life.' Jossy looked more chirpy. 'He looked like a big softie to me.'

'He's actually into American Football,' hissed Tracey. 'He's a line-backer.'

Jossy mumbled something about a 'line-shooter' and urged Tracey and Albert to help with his luggage and the footballs. Tracey hovered.

'You'll find the lads have changed a bit, Jossy.' She gave a glance at Albert. 'And that's not the only thing.'

Albert grabbed the footballs and hurried towards the bus stop. Despite further queries from Jossy, Tracey kept her lips buttoned.

As the bus drew away, Jossy wondered where the music was coming from. Pounding, painful, Wham. Then he saw the flashing rainbow lights inside the shop. He ran forward to look at the sign. It was picked out in chrome: *Magpie Sports Boutique.* Jossy mouthed the words as if chewing castor-oil flavoured gum. Albert cowered, but not Tracey. 'Ace, isn't it? Right up with the times.' She led the way in.

The scene inside the shop was a cross between 'Top of the Pops' and 'The Rocky Horror Show'. Dummies were decked out in every form of plastic and glitter, in everything from roller boots to cycling hats. A strobe light rippled over a kaleidoscope. Down the middle of the shop ran a catwalk and on it Ross Nelson paraded in a purple PVC tracksuit and a velvet tennis visor. His father, Bob, was describing the outfit and what a bargain it was over the microphone. A couple of punters blinked in amazement. Two young lasses, dressed in plastic leotards, came gyrating down the catwalk, ogling Ross.

Jossy was goggle-eyed with amazement. 'I turn me back for a couple of weeks and they've changed me shop into a dance hall.' He rounded on Albert who had scuttled over to join Bob.

'Now don't go throwing a wobbly.' Bob's voice was its usual oily self. (Bob was Glipton's sharpest bookie, and a shrewd judge of business ventures.) He sidled up to Jossy and took his arm. 'Look round. A bit of glitz – the modern look. I suggested it to Albert and . . . your other friends. It's doing a bomb.'

The ring of the till drew Jossy's attention. He looked across the shop and saw Councillor Glenda Fletcher clocking up a sale. Jossy frowned. Glenda was no mug. She was on the Local Council, and had pulled strings for the Giants on the sports committee. *She* seemed to approve of this leap into the modern age, so maybe this new idea deserved some consideration. Glenda swooped. She kissed Jossy lightly on the cheek. Jossy blushed and felt more chuffed than he expected. Maybe his dream on the train was trying to tell him something.

'Great to see you, love. My, you are looking well. You've put on weight in Geordieland.' She pinched at Jossy's waist.

He pulled in his inch or two of midriff bulge. 'I'll admit I had a pint or three – and a few leek dumplings. Get it off in no time.'

By now a couple of customers were lining up at the till. Tracey moved to man it.

'I'm telling you, kidda, you and Albert are onto a winner.' Bob's Geordie accent was atrocious but the point was not lost on Jossy. He moved across the shop to the end of the catwalk where Ross was being lionized by the two girls.

11

'Oh, Ross, you're so cool,' gushed the blonde one.

'Joseph J. Cool to you, Noleen.' Ross turned to Jossy. 'Oh, hello Boss. I felt a right cissy doing this modelling lark at first but it's making business boom.'

Jossy noticed that Ross was definitely overweight and a little out of breath. 'You're not exactly fit, are you, sunshine?'

'What do you expect? There's nobody to train with. They're all . . .' Ross looked at the floor. He seemed embarrassed.

'I don't know what's going on round here.' Jossy was wobbling all right. 'Disco dancing. Male modelling. What's happened to my Giants?'

Albert broke the stony silence. 'As they say, Jossy, one picture is worth a thousand words. Come with me.'

Jossy followed him out of the shop meekly. Ross shouted after them.

'It'll take a strong stomach, Boss, I warn you.'

Louie's Café was a relic of the 1950s in Glipton. The sounds on the juke-box were modern, but the atmosphere was still very much à la Beach Boys. There were booths with red, mock-leather padding on the seats and the Knickerbocker Glory was as designed by Louie himself. It was still a favourite spot for courting couples and it was here that Harvey had set out his stall for his first romantic adventure. It co-starred Opal Twomlow.

Opal sat at a table by the window, intent on fiddling with the laces of the two pairs of skating boots lying by the ashtray. She had on her face an expression of great concentration but in fact there was very little on her mind. Harvey reckoned she was very deep.

He pushed a carton of Super-Slush in front of his beloved. He took a big suck at one of the two straws.

'Strawberry. Your favourite, Ope. Mine too.'

The shadow of a cloud sifted across the hazel eyes.

'I do wish you'd call me Opal.'

Harvey was never slow to exercise his sparkling wit.

'Sorry Opal. You've got to realize I'm 'opeless. Geddit?'

The gag fell on stony ground. But Harvey was never one to be knocked back easily. He took another suck of Slush and gazed round the café. Two familiar faces were peering at him through the glass of the main window.

'A right pair of slush puppies,' said Albert.

Jossy shouted loud enough to be heard inside the café. It even drowned Queen on the juke-box.

'Harvey. Get your nose out of the trough a minute.'

Harvey's eyes rolled in alarm. He tried to cower down behind the skates. Opal cocked a half-interested eye. Jossy continued.

'I want you down the Community Centre for training on Wednesday at six sharp.'

It was in the nature of Richard 'Ricky' Sweet to do things thoroughly. He had been a thoroughly good captain of the Glipton Giants and now he was thoroughly moonstruck. He and Sharon 'Shaz' Gilkes were standing outside Glipton's Computer Corner and the subject top of Ricky's list was a suitable birthday gift for his lady.

'Werewolf Walkabout looks great, doesn't it?' Shaz peered at the game as Ricky thought how nice the shine on her dark hair was. 'And Zombie Blood Spatter would really test the new joy-stick my mum and dad's bought me.' Ricky nodded dreamily. 'You choose, Ricky.'

'Pick one you like, chuck,' murmured Ricky. 'As long as it's in the sale, that is.'

Ricky's hand dipped into the inside pocket of his zipper jacket. He pulled out a chain with a football medallion on it. His voice dripped with sincerity.

'I know we've only been going out a couple of weeks, Shaz. But if you'd wear this, you'd make my happiness complete.'

Shaz did not get a chance to take the chain. With a whizz and a clatter, Albert Hanson's motorbike came to a juddering halt alongside them. Jossy leaned from the sidecar and grabbed the chain.

'The last time I saw this bauble, it was gracing the throat of the lassie who works down the chip shop. Get sick of her, Ricky?'

Jossy's crack had an instant result. Shaz grabbed the chain, pitched it in the general direction of a corporation waste-bin and exited, sharpish.

'You've just mucked up my entire existence, Jossy Blair,' yelled Ricky.

'Girls will always be around, sunshine. Football is a delicate bloom. Enjoy it while you're young and strong. Training. Six. Wednesday. Usual place. Proceed Albert.'

Ricky's further protests were stifled in a cloud of exhaust fumes.

Glenn Rix and Ian 'Selly' Sellick were not as close as they had been. Once, in fashion, football, and life in general, they had been blood brothers, but Melanie Maxwell had put paid to all that. She was Glipton's answer to Madonna and the lads were her greatest fans.

Glenn mooched up to the corner of Canal Street without a glance at the phone-box. In it, two men in caps and macs appeared to be looking up a number. Albert and Jossy's 'disguise' would have fooled nobody except the totally lovelorn. Within seconds Selly had

14

shown up, like Glenn, very smart, and each of them carried a box of Black Magic chocolates. They both tried to hide the boxes.

'Haven't seen you around much lately. Have you been poorly?' Selly was extremely suspicious.

Glenn looked at the paving-stones. 'Well, actually I've been doing a lot of orienteering.'

'I've been studying acupuncture,' muttered Selly.

Melanie hit the scene like Shirley Bassey. She was wearing lots of pale face powder and her nails and lips glowed brightest black. In a different age she would have been slapped straight in the local stocks. She took immediate possession of both boxes of chocolates.

'Thanks. Both of you. I must say that I'm on a diet at the moment. But my mum's been told to eat more – so these won't be wasted . . .'

Glenn and Selly were at each other's throats like fighting cocks.

'Orienteering. You wouldn't know a map from a crisp packet!' hissed Selly.

'Acupuncture! I'll pin your ears together!' Glenn was bristling.

As Jossy and Albert shot out of the phone-box, Melanie departed. Jossy held the pair apart like a boxing referee. His voice was all sweetness.

'Why don't you two use up all this energy down the Centre. At least nobody two-times you at football.'

Glenn went off his own way and Selly his. Jossy's tone was philosophical as he and Albert walked to The British Connection pub.

'I know love can strike anytime, anywhere, but I wish Cupid would steer clear of the football season!'

TWO

The inside of the gym at Glipton Community Centre brought loads of memories flooding back to Jossy. It was here he had first agreed to manage the Glipton Grasshoppers; it was here he knocked them into shape and turned them into the Giants; here the rafters had echoed to cheers when the lads had lifted their first trophy – the Crampton 5-a-side cup. It was all a bit silent now.

Albert paced about near the door. He kept looking at his watch.

'It's turned six, Jossy. I don't think they're going to show up – any of them.'

Jossy was wallowing deep in nostalgia. He was moving the plastic men around his draughtboard, eyes glowing.

'Remember the move that clipped the wings of the Falcons, old son? Ross up from deep, early ball to Selly, Wayne hits a rocket?'

Both of them stiffened as they heard noises in the corridor. Albert looked towards the door with a worried frown, but Jossy's grin was like the sun coming up over a pit heap. He raised himself to his full five foot nine inches. Ricky and Ross led the lads in. Jossy did not seem to notice that none of them was dressed for training – except possibly Harvey and he had a pair of skates over his shoulder.

'You can't whack a hundred per cent turn out for

training.' Jossy's voice was full of enthusiasm. He rubbed shoulders with his lads; a nod here and a playful punch there. 'We've missed two matches and the league's demanding we play at St James's Park on Saturday. So let's get cracking.'

Nobody would look him straight in the face. Albert noticed that most of the lads were dressed for stepping out and that there were a couple of girls hovering in the corridor. Jossy put his arms protectively round Ricky's shoulder.

'I'm planning a new role for you this season, Rick, old son. Piercing runs up front. Just like old Crazy Horse, Emlyn Hughes, used to do.'

'You'll have to ask his squaw about that.' Harvey's gibe raised a few giggles.

Two female faces looked round the door and made google eyes at Des and Billy. Albert flapped a hand and said, 'Shoo'. Jossy's nose began to twitch. He sniffed at Ricky's face.

'Pick up your mum's soap by accident this morning?'

Ricky went beetroot. 'No. It's aftershave.'

'But you don't even have any whiskers yet.' Jossy's humour was not melting any ice.

Glenn and Selly had been edging nearer the door. Melanie was leaning against the door, flashing her talons and looking like one of the brides of Dracula. Several of the others took this as the cue to move out. Jossy scarcely looked at them as they mumbled their excuses.

'I've got to wash my dad's car – honest, Jossy,' was Wayne's offering.

Harvey was twisting about trying to attract Jossy's attention. 'I don't want to seem like a deserter, Boss, but it's half-price down the rink tonight and . . .'

He might have been addressing his remarks to a brick wall. Jossy sat down and began flicking the

17

plastic men around the draughtboard. Ricky, head down, paced to the door and turned round. He tried to make his exit line sound flippant.

'I'm not picking winners anymore, Boss.'

'You're not the only one, son.' Jossy's tone held more acid than a chemistry lab.

Ross was the last to leave. At least he was not racing off after a girl. 'Sorry, Boss. I promise you I'll keep fit and practise ball control – but what's the point? We've no team!'

'Do what you like, sunshine,' was Jossy's flat reply.

Albert did not know what to say as Jossy fished in the hold-all and pulled out one of the new black-and-white striped jerseys. He held it up as if it were the Holy Grail.

'I sweated buckets up in Geordieland getting new gear for this season.'

Albert tried to see a glimmer of light in the darkness. 'Hey, Jossy, with no football to worry about, we can concentrate on Magpie Sports.'

A bit of Jossy's old sparkle rekindled. 'Oh, I'm not going to throw a wobbly. I'll just be patient. Mebbe I can work something out. And, yes, we must think about the business.'

Magpie Sports was fairly throbbing with activity a couple of days later. The sale was proving a success. Tracey pounded the till like a concert pianist; Albert, immaculate in dark suit and maroon tie, ushered the punters around like a past master, and Jossy did the donkey work. His jacket was off, his tie undone and his sleeves rolled up. He was humping boxes in and out of the back room.

'Get another batch of swimsuits out, Jossy. Put them on display and then check the over-sized T-shirt situation.' Albert barked out the orders.

Jossy plonked down the boxes he was carrying. 'Yes, master. Certainly, master. Excuse me, but didn't I once run this place?'

Tracey called Jossy over to the till. 'Slip out and get some sandwiches from the café, will you? I'll have cottage cheese . . .'

'No price!' Jossy's face was set. 'Dogsbody's one thing, but canteen laddie – never!'

Bob Nelson, who had been a firm pillar in the new-style Magpie Sports, walked in with some boxes of snooker balls. He too was looking for a willing hand.

'Albert, I'm off round to the warehouse to collect them exercise bikes. They're a bit heavy, so . . .'

Jossy heeded the call. At least it would mean a breath of fresh air. 'OK, Bob. Say no more. I'm your man.'

Ten minutes after Jossy and Bob had left the shop, Glenn slipped in looking a bit uneasy. Tracey was on him like a ferret.

'Oh, fancy seeing you down here. Melanie given you a day off, has she? Or is she snogging with your better half?'

Glenn shifted from foot to foot. 'Look, just 'cos I'm not a Giant anymore, it doesn't mean I can't come here and help out, does it?'

Tracey was suspicious of this line of chat. She set Glenn fiddling with the window display. It was obvious that Glenn had other things on his mind than helping out. She was even more perplexed when Harvey sidled into the shop and began helping with the window display. It was not long before Ricky, Ross and Selly were also 'helping out', but none of them were saying much. Tracey smelt a rat.

The door clanged and Jossy staggered in with a huge box.

'Errand boy back! Ready and willing to take on more jobs.'

He shut up when he realized that the former Giants were heavily represented on the premises. The lads bent harder to their tasks. Jossy was never one to miss a trick. He walked slowly amongst them.

'I've seen nowt like this since we put on Snow White and the Seven Dwarfs for the school pantomime.'

He started to sing:

'We work, work, work, work,
work, work, work,
We work the whole day through . . .'

He was really getting going when Dave Sharkey's bony figure swooped into the shop. There was an excited flush on his face and his eyes were lit up. The thin lips cracked in an apology for a friendly smile. The smile fooled nobody. Sharkey ran his team, the Ecclestone Express, like a military operation. They were the Giants' bitterest rivals and the two teams had had some real ding-dong battles in the previous season.

'Good afternoon, Mr Blair, and all. My, aren't we all full of busy?'

Jossy glowered as Sharkey went on in his usual pompous manner.

'I seem to see your lads all over Glipton. Their minds don't seem to be on football.' His nose curled slightly as he looked at the boys. 'When I see them they're usually pursuing young lasses. My lads are tuned up nicely for the new season.'

The urge to stick one right on the end of Sharkey's nose almost dominated Jossy. 'Look Dave, if you've come here to crow about our – er – teething problems . . .'

Sharkey butted in. 'Oh no, Jossy, I'm not crowing. In many ways I am an admirer of your football club.

20

Above all, I admire your playing premises at St James's Park.'

Everyone in the shop was now tense. They knew Sharkey was up to something. Ross came in carrying a box of sports equipment. He stopped whistling.

'I have been checking with the league and the Council.' Sharkey took a letter from his inside pocket and flourished it. 'This letter spells out a very serious message for you and your lads, Jossy. It states that if no home game is played by the Glipton Giants by six p.m. on Saturday, then the club loses all claim to the ground. The Express are top of the list to take over.'

The effect of this on Tracey and Albert was like a bomb dropping. But the lads seemed not to care. Jossy's reaction was totally unexpected. He positively strutted over the floor to Sharkey.

'Fancy you taking all the trouble to read the small print, Dave.' He stuck out his bony chin. 'Well, tough luck! Because I've got a team. They'll be showing their paces at St James's at two o'clock on Saturday, so why not pop along? You might get a few tips!'

Jossy's bravado did not fool Sharkey. He strode to the door.

'You're going to need more than bluff this time, Jossy. I will be in vigilant attendance on Saturday. There'd better be a game.'

'No sweat, pal.'

The Giants had heard this cocky tone before, usually when Jossy was onto a hiding to nothing. As he looked round the shop imploringly, nobody would look at him. He dragged Ross into a corner.

'You're a sensible lad, Ross. What can I say to this lot to get them to play? Where's their pride?'

Ross shuffled, eyes down. 'I would play if the others would. But just look at them. Each one eaten up with

21

a burner. Love lost. They'll never be a team the state they're in.'

Jossy could not disagree. The lads definitely did not look bright-eyed or bushy-tailed. Selly was fiddling with the wig on one of the dummies. Jossy tapped him politely on the shoulder.

'Just tell me straight, in your own words, why won't you play?'

'If I spend time at football, Glenn will step in and click with Melanie.' Selly sneered across the shop at his rival.

Jossy marched over to Glenn who was trying on a Chicago Bear's helmet.

'OK, Fridge, or should I say ice lolly? Why have you copped out?'

'Well, now I'm more mature . . .' this made Jossy smile, '. . . I'm interested in women.'

'So what's wrong with a good, healthy activity like football?' Jossy was getting steamed up. 'It'll make you look more attractive.'

'Wrong,' whispered Glenn, 'Melanie's against all forms of aggression.'

Jossy had no answer to this, so he sidled up to Ricky. Gone was the cheerful, freckled face; Ricky looked as though he had the worries of the world on his mind.

'To think that you were once the granite backbone of my defence. Now you're a cross between Oliver Twist and Will-o'-the-wisp off the telly.'

Ricky's words came out as a whine. 'Jossy, I've got this terrible problem. Should I tell my mum and dad that I'm planning on getting married, or should I wait till I'm fourteen?'

Jossy barely stifled a laugh. He moved on to where Harvey was threshing about like a nervous stick insect.

'Ants in your pants, kidda?' asked Jossy.

'No, it's Opal,' Harvey's pain oozed out from every

pore. 'She's smashing to me down the ice-rink, but everywhere else she freezes me out. I've asked her to the pictures, the circus, the zoo . . .'

'The zoo!' gasped Jossy.

'Yeah. I thought her seeing all that animal body language, you know,' he thumped his bony chest like King Kong and let out a Tarzan yell that would not have frightened a dormouse. 'You know – I thought it might make her understand mine. Like – Me Tarzan, you Jane. So how can I get my message across stronger?'

'Sorry, kidda. No easy answers to that one.'

Jossy called Albert over.

'Here, once I was a football manager. Now it seems I'm an Agony Aunt.'

It took a lot to get Jossy Blair down – really down. But this time the Giants had succeeded. A couple of hours after the 'Agony Aunt' session at Magpie Sports, Jossy was sitting in his upstairs flat trying to get interested in 'Tomorrow's World' on the telly.

'Life is much easier when all you've got to think about are machines,' he said to himself, as he switched the set off.

He wondered how to spend the rest of the evening. Albert was off on an outing with his former workmates from the mill. For a moment he thought of popping down to The British Connection, but he decided he'd only get a bigger dose of the blues seeing the happy faces all round him.

The doorbell rang. Jossy jogged down the stairs and opened the door on Tracey. Her face, as usual, was lit up like an angel's and she pressed a warm carrier bag into Jossy's hands.

'My mum's got the baking bug again. Half a dozen home-made sausage rolls.'

23

'Come in, pet,' Jossy practically dragged her up the stairs. 'A right little Miss Cannybody you are, and no mistake.'

Ten minutes later, when they were on their second cup of tea and Jossy had just finished sausage roll number four, Tracey sensed that it might be time to start talking him out of his depression.

'You know your trouble, Jossy?' She didn't wait for an answer. 'You've let the Giants become too important in your life.'

Jossy forgot all about the sausage rolls.

'Don't be daft, pet.' He was obviously put out by the bold statement. 'I'm independent. I can easy get another team.'

'I'm not just on about football.' Tracey's face was deadly serious. 'It's the rest of your life that's adrift. You're rootless. What you need is a real home.'

Jossy was speechless. He had expected Tracey to boost him up a bit but this sounded very like deep criticism of his lifestyle.

'Just look at what the lads are up to.' She now looked extra crafty. 'Chasing girls. Though with their style I don't think they'll ever catch any. Why don't you think of that side of life?'

'You mean – Glenda?' Jossy could hardly get the words out.

'Yes. Exactly. I reckon you'd make a smashing pair. And just think on. If you set your stall out for Glenda, then the lads might get round to feeling neglected.'

Jossy stared into space.

'Marriage, you mean? The whole shooting match?'

'Engagement first.' Tracey's eyes twinkled. 'Then, bull's-eye!'

'I think I'd better sleep on the idea.' Jossy stood up. 'You know, I reckon you're a bit of a psychologist on the sly.'

Tracey walked to the door. 'And Auntie Tracey won't charge you a penny for her friendly advice.'

Jossy gave Tracey time to get to the bus stop before he picked up the telephone. Her lecture had made a few ideas crystallize in his quicksilver mind. He certainly did get some warm, cosy feelings when Glenda was around. So maybe it was high time to do something about it.

'Hello, Glenda, pet . . .'

Once Glenda put on the Frank Sinatra record of 'Strangers in the Night' and slipped into the kitchen to open a bottle of Asti Spumanti, Jossy realized that fate might be on his side. He had shot round to Glenda's house soon after the phone call, pausing only to dab some Brylcreem on his hair. Now he sat nibbling a wholewheat twiglet and planning his campaign. He decided to start with the funnies.

'I must admit that I'm a bit down about the lads packing in football, pet, but there is a funny side to it.' Jossy let Glenda settle nice and close to him on the settee. 'Ricky was on about engagement and even marriage to this Shaz. He'll be asking me how to get a mortgage next.'

A little bit of coyness crept into Glenda's mood. 'Well the birds and the bees catch up with everyone sooner or later, Jossy.'

She flicked her dark hair. Jossy knew that she was a fine looking woman. He could imagine her in a Catherine Cookson novel rising above adversity, black eyes flashing, the full monty. It was time to make his move.

'Do you remember when we first, like, met up?'

Glenda nodded with a warm smile in her eyes.

Jossy continued edgily, 'Well, it was a bit like chalk and cheese . . .'

'You could put it a bit more delicately, Jossy.'

'Me the cheese, of course, mouldy and . . .'

'Full of holes.' Glenda was now jokey. 'And me the chalk – dry and dusty.'

Jossy summoned up all his courage and went for it.

'Well, despite all our battles and sword crossing, I reckon we make a canny team. So, I was wondering, what do you say we get engaged?'

The surprise on Glenda's face suddenly turned to delight. She topped up both their glasses.

'This is very sudden. But I accept.'

She raised her glass and Jossy did the same.

'You're a bit of a scallywag at times, Joswell Blair, but I have admired you for ages. And I must admit you do make my heart flutter.'

'A bit like watching Georgie Best scampering down the wing in his prime.' Jossy began to chant softly. 'Georgie! Georgie!'

Glenda rolled her eyes. 'Not exactly, Jossy. Now, we've got plans to make.'

'Later, pet.' Jossy jumped to his feet. 'It's a night for celebration. Get your coat. I'll take you to the chip shop.'

'You'll take me to the Carvery at The Foresters' Arms, Jossy Blair!'

Jossy picked up his glass. He stopped half way to his lips.

'Hey, the lads will have a blue fit when they hear about this.'

Glenda smiled. 'They won't be the only ones.'

THREE

It did not surprise Tracey Gaunt one little bit that Jossy had taken the plunge. She knew what an impulsive kind of bloke he was. She was sure that Jossy and Glenda would go together like tripe and onions, but he could have played his card more coolly. Now Tracey was working on a wheeze to make Jossy even happier – by getting his team on the ball again. Her chance came pretty soon.

Tracey was minding the shop for Jossy and Albert when Ross jived in with a Walkman in his ears. Snatches of Status Quo filtered out as Ross adjusted the earphones.

'Have you seen Noleen and Lisa?' asked Ross. 'They should be here by now to practise our new modelling routine.'

'They're probably up to their eyes handling your fan mail.'

Tracey did not lay on the sarcasm too heavily. She still quite fancied Ross and she also wanted to lead him along a certain path of action.

'Will you be popping down to St James's Park on Saturday to see Jossy's new team?'

Ross jiggled in front of the full length mirror.

'New team!' he scoffed. 'Only a bunch of mugs would bother with that football lark. Now modelling's fun – *and* it could make me a fortune!'

'I hear some scouts from the big clubs could be round on Saturday.' Tracey threw this information away.

Ross's eyes sparkled. 'Oh, in that case I might slip along. Who's Jossy's new lot playing?'

'Oh, just some scratch eleven,' murmured Tracey.

Ross had not been at the front of the queue when patience was dished out; he got tired of posing and boogied to the door.

'Might see you Saturday, then.' He winked at Tracey. 'Might even take you out sometime.'

'I want thrilling not killing, thank you.' Tracey fiddled with the till until he left.

It was not long before Noleen and Lisa popped in. Tracey told them that Ross had sloped off, but if they played their cards right they could be part of her wheeze. She began to explain . . .

Outside the Glipton Ice Rink, Harvey McGuinn was plugging away at his courtship of Opal Twomlow. A few minutes ago, on the ice, they had been dancing like heaven-blessed lovers; now Opal had gone back into her shell. Harvey wracked his imagination for ways to ingratiate himself.

'Skating doesn't half put a sweat on you, doesn't it?' Polite chitchat was not Harvey's strong point. 'I'll bet you're fair gasping for a milk shake or an ice lolly. Which, Ope?'

Opal, as usual, was staring vacantly into the blue-yellow yonder. 'You choose.'

Harvey shot off to the kiosk as Tracey appeared on the scene. In no time the pair were nattering away like two old fishwives. Harvey returned with an ice lolly to find his true love gone.

'What have you said to Ope? You haven't been upsetting her, have you?'

Tracey looked as innocent as an angel in a nativity play. 'I didn't say nowt to upset her. She said something about having things to do at home.'

28

Tracey took the lolly from Harvey and began to lick it.

'Funny lass, Ope. A bit moody. I never know where I am with her.' Harvey was looking for sympathy.

Tracey nodded. 'You'll soon see her in her true colours.'

The Glipton cinema was showing a movie starring Michael J. Fox and Ricky knew that he was Shaz's favourite actor. But it did not disturb Ricky, since Shaz had assured him several times that he beat Michael J. hands down for looks. Ricky realized there was a certain percentage of flannel in this but he more or less agreed with Shaz's opinion. They were waiting in the queue when Tracey 'happened' along.

'Oh, Shaz, have you a moment?' Tracey's voice was extra polite.

Shaz left the clutch of Ricky's arm. The two girls walked off a few yards, deep in conversation. Shaz kept nodding. The queue started to move forward. Ricky let his feelings show.

'I thought gooseberries were only supposed to pop up in gardens.' He glowered at Tracey.

Shaz rejoined him.

'What was all that about?' snapped Ricky.

'Girl talk,' said Shaz, tapping the side of her nose and giving him a wink.

Glenn and Selly had been spending so much time thinking up ways to foil each other's pursuit of Melanie Maxwell that their fitness was now at an all-time low. Today they had both come to the canal bank looking for the object of their desire and they had found her indulging a new, unusual passion – jogging. It must be said that Melanie was more taken with the head-band and the lurex leg warmers than with any improvement the exercise might afford her body.

The unlikely trio bounded along past the odd narrow boat and the occasional half-submerged supermarket trolley. Glenn and Selly looked daggers at each other.

Tracey pranced into the action like Zola Budd. She high-stepped past the lads with a withering glance and began whispering to Melanie. Whatever ideas she was putting across certainly seemed to appeal. Melanie kept nodding eagerly.

Tracey turned. 'I remember when you two could streak around St James's Park like a pair of cheetahs.'

The boys only glowered at her. Melanie agreed. 'They sound like a pair of ancient bagpipes now.'

The girls stepped up the pace and Glenn and Selly began to labour. Tracey turned yet again.

'Why don't you come along to St James's on Saturday and see Jossy's new team? Cheer them on — if you've got enough breath.'

In the couple of days up to Saturday, the lads did not see much of their girls. Several excuses were dished out: everything from hair washing to catching up on homework. So the lads roamed the streets of Glipton kicking their heels. Without talking much about it, several resolved privately to take their boots along to St James's Park in case Jossy's new team's opponents were short. They also wanted to congratulate Jossy on his decision to get married.

'I can't quite see him in a monkey suit and a cravat, can you?' Ricky put the question to Ross as they approached the 'AWAY' door of the hut.

Ross giggled. 'Glenda will make sure he's at the church. She'll probably chain him to the lich-gate.'

Ricky frowned as he read the notice pinned to the door. It read 'SCRATCH ELEVEN'. He pushed the door open and entered. There were one or two familiar bodies lounging on the benches. Harvey was wearing a tracksuit and a pair of trainers. He seemed ready to play.

'Hey up, look what the wind's blown in!' Harvey's tone was resigned. 'Come to join Jossy's Rejects, have you?'

Glenn and Selly gathered round the newcomers.

'Do you know who's in Jossy's new team?' Selly asked Ricky.

'No idea,' replied Ricky.

'He's probably been round the league pestering the best lads to come and replace us lot.' Ross continued in his usual vein. 'Mind, I'll bet he's got nobody of my class.'

All the boys were a bit touched by the atmosphere of St James's Park. Soon all the ex-Giants were in the dressing-room and changed into football boots and shorts. Nobody said much.

When Jossy walked in, three or four of the lads mumbled congratulations on his engagement. He placed an old hold-all on the floor.

'Well, I can't say it isn't nice to see my old boys back at St James's. It's particularly nice to see you, Ricky.' Jossy's voice turned jokey. 'Still writing to Woman's Own for emotional advice?'

As Ricky blushed, Jossy turned to Harvey.

'How's the love life, kidda? Unfrozen Opal, the Ice Maiden, yet?'

One or two of the others chuckled uneasily. Jossy looked round at them with a funny, serious look on his face. He cleared his throat.

'Look, lads. I want to be deadly serious for a minute or two. Unless a Glipton Giants' team plays a match out there today, Sharkey and the Express will get the ground as their home base. So, straight off, thanks for turning up here prepared to play today.'

There were one or two doubting grumbles.

'You have come to play, haven't you?' There was a strong hint of a challenge in the words.

Jossy did not wait for an answer. He turned the hold-all upside down and a bundle of tatty orange football tops fell out. Again a bit of devilry crept into his voice.

'Some of these might fit. They used to belong to a team called the Grasshoppers – a right bunch of scruffs!'

The lads came forward slowly and picked up their old strips. Jossy made tracks to the door. He turned before leaving.

'Oh, don't let my team's flash new strips put you off. The kit's not paid for yet.'

Ricky stopped for a moment as he pulled on the Number Five shirt.

'It's almost as though he planned for us all to come here today.'

'Well, we're here, so let's get on with it.' Ross made sure all his curls were in place.

A small crowd had gathered at the ground to see Jossy's new team. Bob Nelson was resplendent in a brand new coat with an astrakhan collar. He stood near Albert.

'Shouldn't you be in the dressing-room massaging the new lads?' Bob always found something lacking in other people's behaviour.

Albert shook his head. 'No need, pal. Jossy's got them tuned like catgut. Look, here they come now.'

Jossy led out his new 'lads'. Behind him, Tracey adjusted her captain's armband and bounced a football aggressively. Shaz, Melanie, Opal, Noleen and Lisa moved lithely and purposefully onto the turf. The other girls making up the team looked pretty fit as well.

'I don't believe it!' Harvey was the first of the scratch team out of the dressing-room. 'He's signed up women! Our women!' He copped an eyeful of Opal executing a neat line in dribbling. 'My woman!'

The rest of the team came out and looked round

in amazement. Jossy had the girls interpassing like Argentina.

'Hair washing!' barked Glenn.

'Homework!' whined Selly.

'We've been conned rotten,' hissed Ricky.

On the touchline, Jossy took up his position with a wink to Bob and Albert. Bob thoroughly approved.

'I've got to hand it to you, Joswell. You have well and truly worked a flanker on the lads.'

A snorting and hissing noise behind them announced the arrival of Dave Sharkey. Like the Big Bad Wolf, he huffed and puffed but the house was standing pretty strong.

'What's this farce, Blair?' Sharkey's face had mottled from red to purple.

'Farce, Dave? Farce?' Jossy played his catch like an expert angler. 'If my eyes do not deceive me, out on that pitch is a team in the proud black and white of the Glipton Giants.' Jossy paused for maximum effect. 'And the Scratch Eleven, you will find, are all registered members of the club. Now what do you want, Dave, me and the Committee out there?'

Sharkey reared like a miffed dinosaur. 'You've got me this time, Blair. But take it from me, me and my lads will make you fry this season.'

He stormed off.

The referee blew the whistle for the start of the game. Tracey rolled the ball into the path of Shaz. Her first-time kick surprised all the Giants, most of the spectators – but not Opal. She raced into the area like Maradona on a hat trick. The net bulged behind a boggle-eyed Harvey. A chorus of squeals of delight erupted from the girls. Opal picked the ball out of the net. She nipped Harvey's cheek in a friendly fashion, but it was hard enough to bring tears.

'Opal's cute,' sighed Harvey.

'Yeah. Made to make your eyes water,' quipped Ricky.

None of the ex-Giants laughed.

The lads tried to get their act together. But the combination of lack of fitness and having their heart-throbs as the opposition was too much. Whenever Melanie was near the ball, Glenn and Selly acted like two total strangers instead of twin strikers. Ross did his best but even when Noleen gave him a free shot at goal with a pathetic back pass, he shot wide. It was Ricky, though, who took the biscuit. Shaz, doing a fair impression of a hungry Graeme Souness, clattered Ricky to the floor. As the referee's notebook came out and blood oozed from his shin, Ricky chirped up, 'Shaz, dearest, perhaps I can see you after the match. We can share a bottle of embrocation.'

This remark caused some amusement to Jossy and Company, who were parading the line, shouting 'How-way the lasses'. The final score was 6–0 to the girls. And Jossy was just in the mood to rub it in. At the final whistle, he ordered the girls to stand in line. He approached the boys.

'My team would like to shake your hands, fellas. So if you'd step over and form a line.'

The lads dragged themselves across the field and grudgingly shook hands with the girls. Jossy mooched up behind the boys.

'Just one word about today.' Some of the lads turned. 'Women and football can't mix. But if any of you want to get going as the Giants again, training's at six on Wednesday. Mind, it's going to be tough replacing some of today's team. I'll be seeing you – I hope.'

Ricky and Harvey walked off together.

'He's a right con artist, that Jossy,' said Harvey.

'Never a fault in a manager, son. Never a fault.'

Ricky had the look of a captain about him again.

34

FOUR

Nobody had been happier to see the Glipton Giants back on a football field than Bob Nelson. Certainly he had pushed his son Ross's career as much as possible but now Bob could once more start bragging about the team's prowess down at the golf club on Sunday mornings. As he gunned his Mercedes towards St James's Park a few days after the Boys versus Girls game, he grinned hugely and kept patting the pocket of his tracksuit top. It was typical of Bob that he felt the need to dress up in tracksuit, trainers and headband to watch the lads train. Inspiration, he reckoned.

The lads were definitely in need of some kind of boost. Led by Ross and Ricky, the team straggled round the pitch on the first lap of what was meant to be a training run. Ross suddenly dropped his shoulders and began to walk.

'Come on, pal,' puffed Ricky. 'It's not a nature ramble.'

'It's my nature. I ramble,' hissed Ross.

Ricky pumped his arms and lifted his knees as he came to the gateway where Jossy and Albert were exhorting the team to extra effort.

'Howway lads! It's only the first lap and you look like sunstroked marathon men after twenty odd miles.' Jossy's voice was pained. Ross and Harvey weaved past like a pair of drunks. The next group round flopped helplessly, gasping and coughing.

'Pole-axed!' screeched Albert. 'Flat out after only one lap. You should be ashamed of yourselves.'

Bob Nelson jogged over to the group. The boys sensed that he was very pleased with himself. Those still running broke off and joined the floppers. Bob waited until he had a full audience. He looked at Jossy.

'It's going to take a lot of hard work to get this lot fit for football.' Bob took an envelope from his pocket. 'So I have here a slight incentive, Jossy. Cop this.' He chucked the envelope to Jossy who peeked inside. Jossy's eyes glowed.

'What an operator, Bob!' The lads crowded round Jossy. He held up a ticket. 'I have here tickets for "A Question of Sport" in a week's time.' A buzz ran round the lads. 'It's my favourite programme.'

'Mine too,' said Harvey. 'I get about 80% of the questions right . . .'

'But only 20% of the answers,' shot in Wayne.

Jossy looked archly at Bob. 'But these tickets will only be used as and when a lot of sweat has been expended running round this pitch. Right, Bob?' asked Jossy.

'Right, Boss,' smiled Bob. 'So I think another two laps of the pitch would be just the job.'

There were one or two grumbles, but off the lads went. Jossy winked broadly at Bob.

'Nice one, son. Me and Albert were getting no-where.'

'The value of incentive, Jossy,' said Bob. 'By the way, how are the wedding plans going?'

The smile left Jossy's face. He twitched. 'Canny . . . but steady, Bob.' Jossy did not look him straight in the eyes. 'You can't rush these things, you know.'

Albert looked grave. 'Glenda's a real winner of a lass, Jossy. But don't string her along.'

Bob was looking pretty serious too.

'A bit of tension on the starting blocks never harmed anybody.' Jossy's brightness fooled neither of them. He jogged off after the lads. 'I think I'll do a bit of leading by example.'

Albert and Bob shook their heads. Jossy was going to take some pinning down.

Over the next week the Giants really buckled down to hard training. Most of the girlfriends did not mind, but Opal began giving Harvey a very hard time. Unpredictable as ever, she now claimed that Harvey was neglecting her by going training every night. He carried his tale of woe to Jossy.

'Ever since she smacked a couple of goals past me in that match, she's been as nice as pie. "Harvey, take me to the pictures." "Harvey, do you think I suit these orange legwarmers?" You understand women, Boss. What's her game?' Harvey sat on the shop counter as Jossy locked up on Friday night.

Jossy tried hard to hide a smile. 'They reckon it's a lady's privilege to change her mind, Harvey. Opal's probably the kind who changes it a bit faster than some. So don't let it get you down. Keep your mind on football as well as romance. Don't go overboard.'

Jossy turned to find Harvey gone. Glenda had come in during his bit of friendly advice. The look on her face stopped Jossy in his tracks.

'I was just on my way round to your place, pet,' Jossy gushed. 'There's an Old Tyme Dancing night on down at the Comrades Club. I thought we might cut a rug together.'

Glenda looked more inclined to cut Jossy's throat. 'When people decide to get engaged, certain things are supposed to follow. Like a ring. Then a wedding. You have been decidedly quiet about both.'

'The ring. Of course.' Jossy gave her what he

considered a charming grin. 'I've been so excited about going to "Question of Sport", it plain slipped my mind. We'll go to the jewellers on Monday.'

Glenda moved closer to him, the ice gone from her eyes. 'That's fine. Now, Buttons, you can take me to the ball.'

Glenn and Selly led the Giants into the television studios wearing a banner that read 'Giants support Bryan'. Behind them came the lads, Jossy, Tracey, Albert and Bob, all waving their black-and-white scarves proudly. They were not the only football team represented in the audience. Dave Sharkey and the Ecclestone Express were already in their seats and their banner read 'We're Backing Beaumont'.

Jossy took his seat just a couple of places along the row from Dave Sharkey. He was about to start needling Dave when Bryan Robson of Manchester United and England strode up the gangway.

'Hey up, Jossy,' said Bryan. 'Good to see you, kidda.'

Jossy bathed in the reflected glory. 'We'll all be shouting for you today, Bryan, kidda. Don't let us down.'

'How are the horses treating you?' asked Bryan knowingly.

Jossy looked sheepish. 'I'm laying off.' He whispered it so that Sharkey could not hear. Bryan grinned and went off to his dressing-room.

Jossy noticed that Sharkey had his nose buried in a large book.

'Why have you brought along reading matter, Dave? Do you reckon you're going to get bored?'

Sharkey lowered the tome and looked down his nose at Jossy. 'This is the *Kangaroo Lager Compendium of Sporting Facts*. I intend checking all that proceeds today, round by round. I'm a believer in doing a job right.'

Jossy leaned near Dave. 'What are you going to do if you disagree, chuck the book at them?' He laughed at his own joke. Sharkey did not. Any further banter between the two of them was suspended when the teams came out and David Coleman began the action.

The quiz bug was still burning hot and strong the next day in The British Connection in Glipton. Bob was acquainting himself with the 'Question of Sport' quiz book and Jossy and Albert were airing their knowledge, fortified by crisps and sips of bitter.

'Come on, come on, Bob. Give us one that will really test us.' Jossy was in good form. 'Try me on snooker!'

As Bob flipped through the pages, there was a most unexpected arrival in the bar – Dave Sharkey, spick and span as usual, the effect topped off by a red rose-bud in his lapel. Jossy's high spirits got the better of him.

'Hey up, Dave. Have a drink. Lucozade, is it?'

'Brandy and soda, Jossy.' Sharkey's thin lips curled in a leer. 'Purely medicinal, you understand. He took the quiz book from Bob. 'I'll have you know that I am the sports expert with the Buffalo Brainbox quiz team. You can ask me any question you like.'

A crafty look slid across Bob's face. 'OK, Dave. Which Yorkshire captain did not bat, bowl or field?'

All the regulars put down their glasses and glared at Dave. He paused, preened, then raised his hands. 'Not one of your daft questions, is it?'

'Captain Cook,' said Bob by way of an answer. It got the approval of the public.

'I might have known the Glipton Giants . . .' Sharkey pronounced the words as though sucking arsenic drops, '. . . would lower the flame of knowledge down to the wick.'

Jossy passed Sharkey the brandy. 'There's no need for that attitude, Dave. A bit of fun never hurt anybody.'

It was obvious that something was cooking in Bob Nelson's fertile brain. 'Here, I've had an idea. Seeing as we're all on our toes – and at each other's throats over sport, why not have a contest of brain and brawn between the Giants and the Express?'

The idea clicked.

'We could have a bike race,' said Albert.

'Ball skills down the Community Centre,' added Jossy.

'A *proper* sports quiz,' said Sharkey pointedly.

Bob nodded eagerly. 'It would sharpen the lads up no end.'

Albert had been mad keen to have the bike race but he had not counted on it blocking the course of business at Magpie Sports. Now the news had got round the lads, Tour de France mania had taken over. Albert ushered a couple of punters past Jossy who was explaining the finer points of cycling to Glenn and Selly. The lads certainly looked the part. Glenn was wearing skin-tight silver trousers and Selly had so many spare tyres round his body that he looked like a snake tamer.

'On the flat, lads, sit well back on the seat.' Jossy was balancing a racing bike with Glenn poised on the pedals.

'I don't reckon this, Boss.' Glenn held his posterior a few inches above the seat. 'It's like sitting on a razor blade.'

Jossy ignored this. 'When it comes to hill climbs, the *montagne* bit, as the French say, bend down over the handlebars and pump on the pedals until your eyeballs stick out!'

'We'll have to put extra gel on our hair for stream-lining,' said Selly.

'And we'll need a masseur,' added Glenn.

'The most you'll get from me is a drop of wintergreen on your hocks . . .' Jossy broke off and looked up as the doorbell clanged. Glenda carried her finger with the engagement ring on like the Olympic torch. She bustled into the shop with the light of action in her eyes.

'Jossy, darling, I've just been down at the Vicarage and the Reverend Barnflower has offered us some dates for the wedding.'

As Jossy did his impression of a shrinking violet, Glenda pulled out her diary and began to read. 'How do you fancy the 12th?'

Jossy looked embarrassed. 'No good, pet. That's the cycle cross-country race against the Express.'

Glenda was not pleased. 'The 19th?'

'Ball skills contest. Important, eh, lads?' Jossy tried to involve Glenn and Selly. He failed. They developed a sudden interest in judo jackets.

'The 16th?' The words came from Glenda's mouth like tracer bullets.

'The sports quiz, Glenda, love.' She did not flinch at the dollop of tenderness. Jossy continued, almost pleading, 'I'll need you to coach me. I'll have to be spot on there.'

Glenda's eyes narrowed and she moved nose to nose with Jossy. Bob Nelson came in brightly with a quiz book open but he quickly sensed the atmosphere.

'So this stupid, ego-tripping contest against the Express takes priority over our wedding . . .'

'No, pet.' Jossy's face was grey. 'Don't over-react. I've got to get the lads mentally and physically fit. Isn't that right, Bob?' Bob did not want any part of

41

the squabble. 'We can tie the marriage knot any time,' Jossy bleated.

Glenda's expression was thunderous. 'I know where I'd like to tie it, Jossy Blair. Round your rotten neck.'

She flounced past Bob, who made a desperate effort to cheer up the proceedings. Dipping in his quiz book, he blurted out, 'Where is the Gabba cricket ground?'

'Brisbane,' hissed Glenda. She shot a laser beam look at Jossy. 'Where I might as well be for all you care! If you feel like discussing the timetable for my greatest day,' she paused for effect, 'I'll be at home.'

Glenda left. Jossy looked for sympathy from Bob. 'Women can be very cruel,' was all Bob had to offer.

The Giants' womenfolk pitched in wonderfully to get the lads ready for the bike race. Shaz bought Ricky a book about the *Tour de France* and, even though it was in French, Ricky did his best to read it. Melanie pounded the streets of Glipton in her jogging gear with Glenn and Selly happily in tow. Noleen and Lisa spent gallons of elbow grease on the chromework of Ross's bike. Only Opal let the side down. She had developed a passion for making her own perfume and now spent most of her time in her bedroom, which had taken on the appearance of a chemistry laboratory. This meant that Harvey had been left to his own madcap devices in his preparation for the big day.

Harvey's highly developed sense of self-preservation had come out strongly in his choice of equipment. His Uncle Len had allowed him the use of an old motorbike crash helmet. He had acquired elbow, thigh and knee pads and topped the lot off with a large pair of Biggles-type goggles. At the local scrapyard he had picked up a tricycle with tyres nearly three inches thick. To this he attached a small trailer in which he deposited a full breakdown kit, including a large red triangle.

His arrival at the start of the course a[...] [...] than a little comment.

'Who do you think you are?' asked Ricky, [...] gasp. 'Old Mother Riley?'

Glenn and Selly, sleek and streamlined, stood b[...] their tandem. They began to sing 'Any Old Iron'.

Ross came over, flanked by his fan club. 'You look like you're going camping, not racing.'

Harvey was ready for all the flak. 'I am the only one of our five-man team who has actually walked the course. Cornering is going to be very tricky in some parts. So I have come prepared. My machine is extra stable and I am prepared for every emergency.'

Further banter was prevented by a loud shout from Bob Nelson who was standing by the starting line with an enormous chequered flag. The five Express lads took their places. They were smart, alert, glowing with fitness. Their bikes had even passed the Dave Sharkey test of cleanliness. The Giants looked like a dog's dinner.

Bob dropped the flag. The bikers' muscles bulged. Melanie had been poised to shove off Glenn and Selly. Sad to say she did not know her own strength. Her push was too strong for their legs to keep up with. The tandem capsized.

'Stand back, pet.' Jossy eased Melanie out of the way and helped Glenn and Selly to remount. 'Off you go, lads. Do it for me. It's only two laps of Glipton Woods.'

Sharkey had loomed up like an undertaker. 'I don't know about finishing, Jossy. Some of your lot seem to be having difficult starting.'

'It's early days yet, Dave,' Jossy chirped. 'Early days.'

Twenty minutes later, the first Express lad whizzed past the group at the finishing line on the first lap.

arkey permitted himself an oily grin and a murmur. 'Attaboy, Sawyer. Keep it up.'

There was a swish and a squelch of more tyres and Jossy looked expectantly at the bend. Round came two more Express, one of them using no hands as he waved to the Express supporters. 'Easy, Easy,' rose the chant. Jossy, Bob and Albert began to look worried.

They had every reason. After their initial set-back, Glenn and Selly had combined well on the tandem. But now they had a problem. They had arrived at a stream, beyond which a signpost read *Glipton Dell*. Glenn was puzzled.

'I could have sworn the dell was the other way.'

'You're right,' chipped in Selly, 'What a rotten trick. The Express lads have turned the sign round.'

'We'll show them,' said Glenn.

They began pedalling furiously away from the signpost. The path rapidly became a muddy track, then a bog. They ploughed a furrow a foot deep before slurping to a halt.

Ross was the leading Giant halfway round the first lap. But his love of all things flashy let him down. On a straight stretch of the path, he looked up to see that Tracey was acting as a marshal.

'Come on, Ross. Head down!' piped up Tracey.

Ross took his hands off the handlebars and waved to her. His front wheel hit a rut in the path and Ross sailed off into a bush.

Geography had never been one of Harvey's strong subjects. But when he saw the sign that said *Huddersfield 9 miles*, he knew he was in trouble. The large-scale map he had brought along as part of his emergency pack was not much good, since it had very clearly marked motorways but was a bit thin on woodland tracks.

At one stage on his wandering he had met some

ramblers and they had been astonished to find that he was not all that keen to accompany them along the Pennine Way. Now it was getting dark. Harvey switched on all his lights. Maybe Opal was not that daft, sitting in the house making scent on the cheap. At least she was warm.

At nine o'clock Jossy and company gave up. The five Express lads had doddled the race. Sharkey had gone home beaming. And only Ricky and Ross had got home for the Giants. Jossy's language was unprintable as he led the party home. It was time, he growled, for an inquest.

FIVE

Jossy started the ball rolling at the 'inquest' on the bike race disaster but it was not long before he was forced onto the ropes.

'I'm almost ashamed to be seen out in the streets of Glipton,' Jossy was really laying it on. 'You lot really let the club down. Coming back in the dark, Harvey!'

The arrows began to fly.

'I saw the Express lads carrying their bikes,' chimed in Ricky.

'Me too,' added Ross. 'Nobody told us that carrying the bikes was allowed.'

'Oh, but Mr Nelson and Mr Sharkey told me and the rest of the marshals.' Tracey's voice tapered off as she saw Jossy cringe.

'A little oversight on my part, lads, I'll admit.' His voice rose above the jeers. 'But even carrying the bikes, you lot wouldn't have fared much better.'

Ricky realized that a row would get them nowhere fast. He decided to strike a sympathetic note. 'Look, lads, the ball skills and the quiz are bound to go our way so let's all simmer down.' There were nods and grunts of agreement.

'Boss.' Jossy looked into Ricky's open, honest face. 'You must have a lot of other things on your mind.'

Tracey backed up Ricky's move. 'Have you fixed the wedding date?'

Jossy did not seem keen to answer.

Ross sauntered up to Tracey wearing a serious

46

expression. 'Jossy's down in the dumps because Glenda's giving him the cold shoulder.'

He was amazed at Tracey's reaction. Her eyes flashed and she hissed. 'You lot don't help him much. He's got to wipe your noses for you. You mucked up the bike race. Heaven knows what fools you'll make of yourselves in the ball skills and the quiz.'

Jossy had gone into the back room to sort out some stock. He got a bit of a shock when he received the first of several deputations. Glenn and Selly came in looking very sheepish.

'We're sorry we screwed up the cycling, Boss.' Selly looked crestfallen.

'We thought we could do the job better together.' Glenn leaned forward and clutched Jossy's arm. 'Think on it – all partnerships have bust-ups at times.' The lads nodded like a pair of wise old monks. Jossy shook his head as if dreaming. They left.

Harvey sloped in like a spy about to pass over the top secret plans. 'I just want to say, Boss, that I'm sorry I got lost in the woods. You've got to realize that sometimes enthusiasm runs away with people. Make allowances.' It ran through Jossy's mind as Harvey slunk out that maybe the detour round the woods had caused Harvey to lose some of his marbles.

Ross bounced in. 'I'm off to practise my ball skills for a couple of hours, Boss.' He leaned forward with a wink. 'Why don't you sit down with your diary and get your wedding date nailed? Leave the footie to us.' He strutted out, leaving Jossy gaping like a guppy.

Ricky did the whole Sir Laurence Olivier touch: hand on breast, the works. 'I'm the captain of this club, Boss, and I've let you down. I'm mature enough to know my responsibilities – just like you have to shoulder yours. It took you a long time to see that Glenda was just the girl for you, but we knew – deep down.' He paced out.

Jossy looked at himself in the mirror over the sink. 'It's getting like the Marriage Guidance Council round here, kidda. And I'm not even married – yet!'

Johnnie the Runner's spidery writing was occasionally very hard to read but Jossy made out the last bit of the letter clearly. '*All the very best, Johnnie. P.S. Kilkenny Crystal is a racing cert for the three o'clock at Fairyhouse on Wednesday. Go on, be a devil.*'

It was Wednesday today so, somewhat furtively, Jossy picked up the paper and turned to the racing pages. Kilkenny Crystal looked a good investment at 8–1. It did not take long for Jossy to convince himself that it was his lucky day. He wrote the words *Kilkenny Crystal* down on a strip of paper. He put down his mug of tea and walked from the back room of Magpie Sports into the shop.

'Just popping out to get *The Post*, Albert.' Jossy jogged to the door. 'I'm looking at the housing market.' Albert barely looked up from a catalogue of sports gear.

Mentioning the housing market set Jossy thinking about his forthcoming wedding to Glenda. After the ball skills and the quiz contests against the Express, he would really buckle to and fix the date, etcetera. He decided that he was really looking forward to the advantages of married life: good food, companionship, somebody to talk over the Giants' tactics with. He was miles away as he arrived outside the bookies.

'Not going in there to place a bet, I hope.' Glenda's voice pulled the rug on Jossy's reverie.

'Well, hello pet. I've just been thinking about our plans.' Jossy laid on the charm like breakfast marmalade while at the same time trying to hide the piece of paper. His mention of plans deflected her attention.

'So you have been thinking about us,' there was a tinge of hurt in her voice.

'Of course, pet.' Jossy had a brainwave. 'The lads want to club together and buy us a present. They've suggested Kilkenny Crystal.' He opened the slip of paper. Glenda looked impressed. 'Albert says it's the best. Sparkles like moonlight on the Tyne.' Glenda's eyes glowed. 'I was just on my way to the shops to clock some.'

Glenda looked to be on the verge of tears. 'Oh, how touching. And here's me thinking you were getting cold feet.'

'Chance would be a fine thing.' Jossy pecked her on the cheek. 'I know when I'm well off, kidda. What a pair we'll make.'

'I've got a committee meeting at three prompt, Jossy,' said Glenda, eyeing her watch.

'Hurry along then, flower.' Jossy gave her another peck.

As Jossy watched her disappear around the corner by the bank, the tannoy crackled inside the bookies. 'And here at Fairyhouse the going is firm. Kilkenny Crystal is now 12–1 and looking lively . . .'

'. . . and sparkling, I hope,' whispered Jossy, as he shot inside.

There was an atmosphere like Wembley Stadium on Charity Shield day in Glipton Community Centre as the Giants and the Express trotted out for the football skills contest. The Giants' girlfriends, after soundly thrashing the lads at soccer, were now giving one hundred per cent support to the team. Shaz was wearing a Magpie striped top hat. Melanie had knitted a black and white scarf that could comfortably have gone round her, Glenn, Selly and Glipton Town Hall. Noleen and Lisa were kitted out as cheerleaders. Even Opal had caught the team spirit to some degree; she was wearing black glasses and a white bobble hat.

'She's posing again, that Opal,' was Ross's sly

comment as he jostled to the front of the crowd at the football tennis area. Glenn, Selly and Wayne lined up for the Giants and very soon went into a 3–0 lead.

'Howway, lads. Keep it up,' bellowed Jossy, who was feeling in fine fettle. Kilkenny Crystal had indeed sparkled and Jossy was twenty-four pounds better off as a result. He had not done much bragging about it in case news got to Glenda's ears.

Jossy crossed the hall to the cone-dribbling area and began the verbal assault again. 'Come on, Ricky. Eye on the ball.' Jossy's eye was on the door. He was not keen to be harassed again by Glenda seeking precise details of the wedding arrangements.

'Come on Express. Concentrate!' Sharkey was working up a fair head of steam as his player knocked over a cone. Ricky finished the course well ahead. There was a big cheer when it was announced over the tannoy that the Giants' trio were 11–7 up at half-time in the football tennis.

It was not in Jossy's nature to miss an opportunity to gloat. He sidled up to Sharkey. 'Bit different to pedalling round Glipton Woods, this, Dave, old pal. This takes skill.'

Sharkey bared his teeth as if he was auditioning for a role in 'Jaws III'. 'Even if my team fail in this – er – circus today, Blair, we'll demoralize you when it comes to intellect.'

'Your big time small talk sounds fine, Dave. But if I were you I wouldn't bet on winning the quiz.' Jossy looked smarmy.

'Will you be able to leave the betting shop for long enough to take part?' was Dave's sarcastic thrust.

Jossy did not stay long enough to parry. He sniffed and headed for the goalkeeping contest. The idea here was that each team's goalie faced five shots from the opposition. Harvey was poised like a cat on the line.

50

Jossy noticed at once that Harvey's eyes were not on the ball. They were on Opal, who was chatting away to the very handsome older brother of an Express player. Jossy beckoned the lad over.

'You don't want to go chatting up Opal, son, not unless you want to get your face rearranged.' Jossy sounded like a favourite uncle.

'How do you mean?' asked the lad.

'Well, you know Rambo Kellett, the England Youth Rugby League player,' Jossy mimed a gorilla. 'Well, Opal's his bird. And he'll be here in a minute, after he's finished his weight training.'

The lad blanched and moved off quickly. Jossy stood by Opal.

'What did you say to Carl?' asked Opal, huffily.

'He was thinking of backing a horse. But I convinced him it would be a loser.' Jossy's voice was all sweetness. 'Come on, Harvey!'

Harvey did the business. He hurled himself about like a jumping cracker. The other lads crowded round the goalie event bearing news of wins in the other two contests.

Jossy relaxed, knowing that it did not matter how Harvey performed now. Lovely day, he thought. Lads on song. Kilkenny Crystal on song.

Glenda too was on song. 'Oh Jossy, Jossy dear,' she trilled as she ploughed through the throng. Jossy turned with a broad smile. Glenda continued, 'Silly me, I've got no change for the parking meter. Can you help me, love?'

Jossy dipped his hand in his pocket and pulled out loose change, four fivers – and the betting slip from the bookies. Glenda froze when she saw it.

'I knew you were pulling a fast one about Kilkenny Crystal, Jossy Blair.' She was furious. 'Lying to me – and gambling!'

Jossy knew when he was beaten. 'It won, pet,' he almost grovelled.

'I should have known.' Glenda murmured the words, but they struck home. Before Jossy could react, she was out of the hall.

Albert and Tracey bounced over from the football tennis.

'It's a great day, Jossy. Victory all round.' Albert did not sense the mood.

'What's up, Jossy?' Tracey, as usual, was right on the ball.

'I'm afraid my past has caught up with me a bit,' said Jossy. 'And it's casting quite a shadow over my future.' He brightened. 'So, what are we doing all standing around here? Ricky, Ross, lads. We'll have the eliminators for the quiz in the shop on Wednesday evening. So start hitting the books. Tracey! You're Quiz Mistress.'

Tracey nodded. But Glenda's sudden exit worried her. Jossy's ship of love seemed to have entered yet another stormy passage.

Ricky Sweet was known to his mates as a bit of a swot when exam time came round at school. But he was nothing compared with Shaz Gilkes. She was determined that Ricky was going to be in the Giants' team of three for the quiz and she had made Ricky worm away at the books for hours. Now, as the crowd gathered for the trials, she was still rabbiting on.

'Don't leap in with an answer too quickly, chuck,' Shaz droned on. 'Pause, select, then strike confidently.'

Ricky wished she would shut up but he smiled politely as he watched Harvey prepare to air his knowledge.

The shop was in almost total darkness except for the light from an anglepoise lamp pointed at a black leather

'Mastermind' chair. Tracey, Bob and Albert sat at a table opposite like the Spanish Inquisition, columns of reference books rearing up beside them. Tracey approached the chair with a list of questions.

'I am your question person this evening and I welcome you all here. We are after the three brightest sparks in our club,' Tracey did not look too confident about finding them, 'And I want no smarthead cracks to spoil the proceedings. Remember, Sharkey and the Express will be taking this dead serious.'

'Hear, hear, pet,' Jossy looked up from the *Guinness Book of Records*. 'I'm awash with sporting facts.'

'So we should make a clean sweep. Geddit – awash – clean.' Harvey was obviously in fine form. He took his place on the hot seat.

Tracey read out the question. 'What sport was invented by North American Indians?'

Harvey frowned, then beamed his usual silly grin. 'Rhythmic scalping?'

Tracey's whiplash tone showed what she thought of the attempted joke. 'Wrong. The answer is lacrosse. Shift, Brainbox.'

Harvey shuffled off and Ross took his place. He patted his curls. 'Ross Nelson, reading Machismo.'

'Fat chance,' muttered Tracey. 'What do you have to be to qualify to play cricket for Yorkshire?'

'Handsome?' Ross looked at Tracey with what he fancied was charm.

'Frame yourself, son.' She was not biting.

'Trendy?' The gallery merely shuffled.

'I'll give you five more seconds,' said Tracey.

'I don't know. A fan of Emmerdale Farm?' Ross's pathetic performance had got the crowd going.

The laughing and giggling did not please Tracey. 'You have to be born in the county. Next.'

During the next quarter of an hour the Giants

plumbed almost incredible depths of ignorance. Tracey was horrified at the stupidity of the boys. Nobody had yet got a question right and there was only Ricky and Jossy still to go.

'Come on, Genius, show them what you're made of.' Jossy patted Ricky on the head as he walked to the front. He shouted to Tracey, 'Give me any question you like about snooker and football.'

'Your mind blank about horses and greyhounds?' Tracey could not resist the dig.

Jossy looked at her as though she was a mass murderess. She turned to Ricky.

'General knowledge for you. What wonder of the Ancient World is thought to have stood at the harbour mouth of the island of Rhodes?'

Ricky's freckled face creased up with concentration.

'I don't think he's going to get it.' The shrill voice sounded confident. 'The answer is the Colossus.' Glenda had entered and was in the mood for making her presence felt.

'What's she got to stick her nose in for?' Wayne was not the only one angry. Jossy bristled, but decided to say nothing.

'I didn't know the answer, anyway,' said Ricky.

As he was about to leave the chair, Tracey stopped him. 'The light of learning is burning very dim around here, Ricky, and you're a genius compared with the rest of this lot,' Tracey whispered, then pushed Ricky back into the chair. 'Which football team plays at Craven Cottage?'

'Fulham!' shouted Ricky.

Jossy almost did a lap of honour. Glenda had moved nearer to him but now he was over by the chair, clapping Ricky on the back.

'Great, Rick! What a team. We'll have me, you and . . .' Jossy hesitated.

'That's just the point, Jossy.' Tracey's voice was harsh. 'Who else?'

'Not her,' Ross yelped, pointing at Tracey.

'No, not me,' Tracey sneered at them. 'But can I suggest that we agree with the Express that the quiz teams shall comprise two club members and a special guest.'

'Great idea, Tracey.' Jossy picked up one of the sports books and began beavering – for racing questions.

Glenda's voice rang out again, crystal clear. 'On what date in the very near future will Jossy Blair be getting married?'

The words hit like a thunderbolt. Everyone stopped talking. Typically, Jossy tried to brazen it out. He read out loudly from the book. 'Who knows which England cricketer was known as the "Master"?'

'Jack Hobbs.' Glenda's words came out softly. They hung in the silence. 'And, I repeat, name the date of Jossy Blair's wedding?'

Bob's bouncy arrival did little to lessen the tension. But Jossy made the most of it.

'Hey up, Bob. Great to see you.' Jossy wrapped his arms around Bob like he was a long lost buddy. 'We've decided that each team in the quiz would have a special guest.'

'You mean me, Brainbox Bobbie?' Bob looked like a happy spaniel.

'No. I've got you marked down as Quizmaster. That's Bob's spot, isn't it, Tracey?'

Jossy looked at Tracey, appealing. Her eyes were on Glenda who had slowly walked to the blackboard used for weekly tactics discussions. Glenda picked up the chalk and wrote in capitals, *JOSSY'S WEDDING – THE 5TH!*

Head high, she paced to the door. Before leaving, she mouthed quite clearly to Jossy, 'Or else!'

55

On the night of the quiz the gym at Glipton Community Centre was doing a fair impression of the 'Question of Sport' studio. On the stage were two desks for the contestants and in the middle Bob had really gone over the top as host and Quizmaster. He was dressed in an old-fashioned evening suit with wide lapels. At his throat he had a large velvet bow-tie and his hair gleamed with Brylcreem. He had piles of question cards in front of him and a huge dinner gong for the timed sections. By his side sat an embarrassed Albert who had been elected chief facts verifier.

About sixty people made up the audience: Giants, Express, girlfriends, cronies and one or two parents. They were making a fair racket with chants for their heroes when Bob started his own act.

'Good citizens of Glipton, calm down and hush your noise. We now come to the final of our three-part test of mind and body. The Express won the cycling race and the Giants the football skills. So tonight's test of brains is the decider.' The crowd cheered. Bob continued. 'Despite the seriousness of the occasion, I have a joke for you.' There was a chorus of groans. 'Did you hear about the brainy fly catcher? He was always swatting!' Bob waited for a reaction. None came. 'Geddit? Always swotting!' Bob waved his hands furiously. There was still not so much as a titter.

'Get on with it, Bob, before they all go home!' was Albert's blunt advice.

Bob cleared his throat and banged the gong for order. 'Right. I shall introduce two members of each team first, then I shall call on the special mystery guests.' A buzz ran round the audience, since nobody knew who the guests were. 'For the Express, a man respected in circles far beyond the centre circle,' again Bob waited for a chuckle, again he got none, 'the club manager, Dave Sharkey! And, backing him up, the

Express captain, Jason Burnbrook.' The Express pair took their places to polite applause.

'Next,' Bob was really into his stride now, 'reading Racing Form and Credit Betting – Jossy Blair. And a micro-chip off the old block, Ricky Sweet.' Jossy and Ricky waved to the audience and sat down. All four of the contestants looked expectantly at the gap in the curtain where the mystery guests would come through.

Bob's manner changed from jovial to arch. 'Now to the first mystery guest. She's a notable figure in our community and she is a committee member of the Giants.' Bob paused for his words to sink in. There were some stunned faces in the crowd but Jossy took the cake. He was blitzed. Bob continued, 'Adding glamour to the Express line-up, Glenda Fletcher!'

Glenda bounded through the curtain like Boudicca doing a lap of honour after a chariot race. She shook Jason's hand, kissed Sharkey on the forehead and gave Jossy a withering glance. The crowd rumbled.

'And completing our line-up, thanks to sterling work by Tracey Gaunt of the Giants, we have a veritable titan of English football – would you please put your hands together for England's captain – Bryan Robson!'

This produced uproar. The Giants began to sing 'You'll Never Walk Alone', Sharkey's face twisted as if he were chewing razor blades and the grin came back to Jossy's face.

'You've worked a few flankers in your time, petal, but this one takes the biscuit,' he yelled at Tracey.

The next half hour kept the crowd well entertained. Glenda and Sharkey combined cleverly, especially on the general knowledge questions. Jossy and Bryan shone, sparkled and occasionally flannelled to good effect. With only three questions to go, the score was Express 23, Giants 21. Bob put the next question to the Giants.

'Who defended the World Heavyweight boxing title on the most occasions?'

Bryan was in like a whippet. 'Joe Louis!'

'Right,' said Bob. 'Express. Which is the oldest football club in the world?'

Jason and Glenda exchanged puzzled looks. Sharkey closed his eyes and put his fingertips to his temples. The crowd hushed.

'Corinthian Casuals?' Sharkey was none too sure.

'Wrong!' said Bob. He looked at Jossy, then Bryan, confident that these two soccer pundits would have the answer. Two blank faces stared back at him.

'Sheffield FC, founded 1857,' Ricky chirped out the answer confidently.

'Right!' yelled Bob. Jossy and Bryan hugged Ricky.

'Brilliant, sunshine.' Jossy was ecstatic.

'That makes the score 23 apiece!' Bob milked the atmosphere for all it was worth. 'Right. The last question goes to the Giants first. If they get it wrong, I pass it over to the Express. Here's the question – What was the score in the Youth International, England against Bulgaria in 1966? No verbal conferring!'

Ricky, as team captain, frowned. Jossy began flapping his hands excitedly. Ricky thought Jossy was joking as usual. 'You answer, Bryan,' muttered Ricky.

'I'd say, as a guess, two-nil to England.' Bryan smiled, hopefully.

'Wrong!' shouted Bob. Jossy threw his head in his hands.

'Express. Any ideas?' Bob looked at Jason.

'Two-one to England?' Jason was obviously guessing.

'Wrong again,' said Bob. 'It was . . .'

'Three-one to England!' Jossy's voice stopped the crowd's buzz.

'Right!' said Bob.

'How on earth did you guess that?' squeaked Ricky.

'Guess!' Jossy growled at him. 'I only played in that match. And I only scored the second goal. Lovely header it was!'

Above the clamour, Bob's voice rang out. 'So I declare the quiz and the overall contest a draw.'

The two teams were given a generous round of applause. Jossy crossed to shake Sharkey and Jason by the hand. As he passed Bob he slipped him a piece of paper. Glenda refused to look in Jossy's direction. She sat stock still, stony-eyed. Jossy tried to keep cool as he looked across at Glenda. Her expression, like a little girl lost, made him want to run across and cuddle her.

Bob stood up and calmed the multitude. 'Before you all go shooting off to the chip shop or the pub – or lover's lane – I have an announcement to make. Although two of our eminent panellists, Glenda and Jossy, have been locked in mortal combat this evening, they have decided on a day to tie the knot as man and wife.'

It was as if an electric shock had run around the Giants.

'She's nailed him!' whooped Wayne.

Glenda's face melted into a soppy smile. Jossy looked as though he had just been made Manager of the Month.

Bob gushed on. 'The date will be . . . the 28th of next month.'

Applause broke out around the hall. Sharkey offered his hand to Jossy. Tracey moved to Glenda's shoulder.

'Congratulations,' she whispered.

'I trust you will be bridesmaid, dear,' Glenda was almost in tears.

'Yes,' said Tracey. 'But not if the groom is going to turn up with a rosette and a black-and-white bobble hat!'

SIX

Over the next few days Cupid played a blinder as far as the Giants and their manager were concerned.

Ricky had really got hooked on the quiz lark. He joined a team called the Knowsley Know-alls and they were taking part in friendly contests prior to forming a league. Shaz was acting as his coach, peppering him with questions as they wandered hand in hand by the canal.

Harvey had at last found something that rippled the pond of Opal's normally blank mind. She was a different person when she played 'Trivial Pursuits'. So Harvey spent long hours airing his sketchy knowledge of all subjects under the sun and doing his best to let Opal win. It was not difficult.

Glenn and Selly had resolved their differences over Melanie. She had persuaded them to leave behind most of their punk image and try out whatever trend attracted her butterfly fancy. The week after the quiz she was into the Beach Boys look, so the lads trailed around after her like two surfers looking for a missing board.

Ross took Tracey out a couple of times. They spent most of the dates discussing Jossy and Glenda's wedding, but Tracey thought she detected a spark of something there. She was not sure what to make of the situation. It was probably best if she and Ross stayed good buddies.

But the front runners in the romance stakes were definitely Jossy and Glenda. There was no doubt that Jossy was setting out his stall good and proper. He was even taking Glenda out wining and dining. The Taverna Neapolitana was half way down Glipton's main street and it was a Mediterranean island of colour and noise. From the walls blazed pictures of Capri and Venice and in pride of place was a photograph of the Italian World Cup squad of 1986, with the slogan *Forza Azzuri*, which Jossy assured Glenda was the Italian for 'Howway the Lads'. Dreamy mandolin music was piped to all parts. As Glenda dabbed at her lips with a red serviette, Jossy attacked the last of his spaghetti course with spoon and fork.

'Twist it round your fork, dear. It's not rice pudding,' hissed Glenda.

Jossy paused in mid chew. 'Why Italians have got to eat string, I don't know. This is pasta joke!'

Glenda held her glass of wine up to the light. '*La dolce vita*. Don't you just love it, Jossy. Wine, food, romantic music. The Latin nations, especially the Italians, know how to live.' She sipped the wine. Jossy finished his spaghetti and a waiter took away the plates.

'I hope he remembers to bring the tomato sauce,' said Jossy.

'You are not, repeat not, putting ketchup on the steak pizzaiola, Jossy!' hissed Glenda.

'Just a joke, pet.'

Glenda melted. 'We must go to Italy for our honeymoon, dear. You'll love it.'

Before Jossy could answer, the manager glided up to their table. He was a very macho type with lots of gold bits on his hands and neck.

'How was the starter? You like?'

'Canny.' Jossy was determined to get his two penny-

61

worth in. 'Not a patch on leek dumplings mind, but canny. You will make sure that my steak's well done?'

Glenda's voice reeked of politeness. 'And I hope there'll be not too much garlic in my Veal Vittoria – just a . . .'

'Teeny-weeny bit,' oozed the manager.

As he turned to go to the kitchen, Jossy chipped in again. Pointing to the poster, he said, 'I see you've got Altobelli and the lads in pride of place.'

The manager blew a kiss to the poster as Jossy ignored Glenda's frown. 'Azzuri. The Blues. Fantastic!'

'They didn't exactly set Mexico alight,' Jossy's voice was as dry as a stick. 'They gave very little cause for cracking the Chianti back home.'

Glenda almost spilled her wine. The manager was not pleased either. He pushed his face right up to Jossy's. 'What do you know about football, signor!'

'A fair bit,' bragged Jossy. 'I'll have you know that I'm the manager of the Glipton Giants FC. Best boys' team in the area.'

'Little boys.' The manager said it as though they were vermin. 'I bet you change their nappies real good!'

Before Jossy could return the insult, the manager swept off into the kitchen.

'Oh, very mature, I must say. Exchanging silly insults over football,' Glenda bristled.

'He started it,' rapped Jossy.

'Yes, and you'll get him at playtime,' chided Glenda.

The manager swooped to their table with the main courses. He grovelled as he put down Glenda's plate. But Jossy's landed like a discus. 'Steak Pizzaiola. Well done.' He gave a sarcastic bow. 'Philistine.'

Jossy prodded the steak with his fork. 'Stone me, pal, this is still alive!'

'Those are the natural juices coming out, sir. Any more well done and it would be a hamburger. No taste.' The manager ground his teeth.

'He's right, Jossy. I'd say that was cooked to perfection.' Glenda was trying to be the soul of tact.

Jossy stood and picked up the plate. 'Take this back to the kitchen and put it under the grill for another ten minutes.'

The manager gave Jossy the sort of look you give maggots in cheese. 'I will not insult my chef!'

Jossy put down the plate, which was hot. Still standing, he wagged a finger at the manager. 'You know nowt about cooking, sunshine.'

'And you know nothing about football.' The manager's expression changed. 'Here, I tell you something. My cousin runs a boys' football club and in one week his team, the Sorrento Salvos, are coming here on tour. How about they play your bambinos?'

Jossy sat down. He looked thoughtful. He cut a piece of his steak. 'You're on, pal. How about that, Glenda? The Giants going international.'

Glenda was tucking into her veal, glad the barney was over. 'Splendid, Jossy. Now eat!'

Jossy speared a piece of steak and popped it into his mouth. 'Magnifico!' he cried. 'My compliments to the chef.'

The manager smiled. 'To play your boys, the Salvos will need accommodation for a night or two. You can fix?'

'No problem,' murmured Jossy.

Jossy had summoned all the lads to the shop without a peep about the Italian job. Now he stood behind the counter, sporting a king-sized grin as the Giants assembled.

'What's up, Boss?' asked Harvey. 'Another quiz?'

'No,' Jossy sounded businesslike. 'Our next project will be more physical than mental. But, now you've mentioned a quiz, here are a few pertinent questions.' The lads looked stumped. 'What is Italy famous for?'

'Leather shoes?' was Selly's best effort.

'Ice-cream,' said Wayne, licking his lips. 'Tutti-frutti.'

'No, dummies, Italy is famous for football.' All the boys nodded. Jossy bobbed down behind the counter and came up with a pile of magazines. 'Here, lads, Italy's top football magazine.' He began dishing out copies. 'Read and learn. You're going to need all the gen you can get.'

Ricky looked at the pictures and words on the inside. 'Nobody more willing to learn than me, Boss. But how can I? It's in Italian!'

'Get a dictionary,' snapped Jossy.

Harvey glanced at a picture of Paulo Rossi. 'What do we want to know about Italian football for?'

Glenda, who had been mucking about in the back store room, was at her most acid. 'Because during our quiet, romantic Italian meal the other night, your manager fixed up a match with the Sorrento Salvos before the sweet trolley came round!'

Jossy nodded. 'We are going to be hosts in a matter of days to the Sorrento Salvos. My mate Luigi down the Tav Nap . . .'

'Mate! You were nearly exchanging blows!' Glenda exclaimed.

'. . . my mate Luigi has a cousin Vito who is manager of this team. They want an extra fixture. So we're it.'

A cheer went up from the lads. It seemed an ace idea all round.

'I want a couple of special training sessions before

the big game. OK?' Jossy did not foresee any aggro at this suggestion.

'Right on, Boss.' Ricky was in a good mood. 'What shall we train on? Bolognese crisps?'

'Funny!' said Ross. 'I'll run rings round the Italians, Boss.'

'I don't think we should be too cocky,' warned Jossy.

Albert had just finished putting the Giants through their paces in the gym. He called for ten final squat thrusts.

'Give us a break, Albert. My arms are going to snap,' gasped Ross.

'One – and thrust – and two – and thrust . . .' Albert snapped out the rhythm. Jossy nodded approval as he set up the blackboard for a quick burst of tactics. The lads creaked and groaned to the end of the exercise.

'OK, blossoms, over here on the double. Chop, chop.' Jossy clapped his hands impatiently. The lads struggled over.

Jossy wrote the words *Sorrento Salvos* on the blackboard. He turned away from the board like a pompous teacher about to lecture a class on his pet subject. 'Note this well. With the Salvos, as with the Italian national team, the emphasis will be on a highly skilled, highly mobile – indeed orchestrated – defence.'

'I've got de nails, I'll mend de fence!' joked Harvey.

Jossy gave him a withering glance. He chalked several crosses over the goal and drew an arrow across the goal area. 'The usual form of Italian defence is *catenaccio*.' Jossy wrote something approximating to the word on the board.

'*Catenaccio!*'

'Sounds like a sauce you pour on chicken,' suggested Wayne.

'To beat this sytem we need strong forward runs at

65

the defenders. OK?' Jossy looked at a sea of blank faces. Tactics never had meant much to his lads. They took his waved arm to mean it was time to pack in. They began to sprint for the door.

Albert tapped Jossy on the arm. 'Hey, you forgot to mention accommodation.'

'Lads!' Jossy bellowed and the boys turned. 'I want to know tomorrow night who amongst you can put up one of these Italian lads. All they want is some grub and a kip. They don't want luxury.'

The meeting about billeting the Italians was going strong. Jossy, Albert and Glenda stood by the till and Tracey was making a list of who could take a lodger. Selly was explaining why he was unable to help. 'It's all my skiving Uncle Cedric's fault. He came from Cleethorpes for a weekend eighteen months ago and he's still here.'

'Understood,' said Tracey. 'That means six Italians still have nowhere to stay.' She was about to add something but Bob's entrance was flamboyant, even by his standards. He had overheard the problem.

'Whatsa matter your face?' lilted Bob. Tracey raised her eyes to the ceiling. Ross blushed. Bob was dressed like a Chicago gangster: white suit, white tie, black shirt. On his head was a wide-brimmed trilby hat and he was wearing shades. 'Bobbi Nelson, he say he take two boys.' Bob broke into his normal voice. 'I could take the team manager and one of the boys. They'd be at home with us – I've got Italian blood you know.'

'First I've heard,' muttered Ross.

'Good idea, Bob. You can take the manager, Vito Cellini. Maybe he's in the Mafia too,' Jossy grinned.

Bob jumped a mile. 'Cellini. Did you say Cellini? I've got relatives by that name in the olive oil business

66

and they live in Sorrento. This geezer is probably family.'

'Real cosy,' said Albert.

The door clanged and in walked Opal, Shaz and Melanie. Opal was carrying an English-Italian dictionary and the girls had a conspiratorial look about them. Harvey waved to Opal but was ignored. Shaz did not look Ricky in the eye. Melanie was too busy practising Italian phrases to even look at Glenn and Selly. The boys were miffed.

'So, we still have to find a roof for four of the lads,' Tracey's voice was firm.

'My mum and dad say we can take one,' said Shaz, still looking away from Ricky.

'Mine too,' Melanie looked delighted at the prospect.

'My sister's gone on a field trip,' Opal chipped in. 'So I'll have one as well.'

'And my mum says we can squeeze one in.' Tracey spoke with a sidelong glance at Ross.

'I think it's perfectly splendid of you girls,' Glenda gushed.

Jossy nodded. 'So, when the bus hits Glipton Market Place tomorrow, you pick out the Italian you like the look of.'

'Oh, yes,' said Opal, Shaz and Melanie. Then, giggling together, they left the shop.

Ricky thumped a punch-ball he was standing near. Harvey looked stunned. Glenn blamed Selly's Uncle Cedric.

'Italians are courteous, charming and friendly, boys. Don't worry.' Glenda smiled brightly, but Jossy did not look too sure.

SEVEN

Glipton had seen nothing like it since the Queen's Silver Jubilee celebrations. The Giants, officials, hangers-on and girlfriends had turned out in force in the Market Place. A couple of banners had been printed; they read *Giants salute the Salvos*, *Buon Jorno Bambinos*. Several of the lads had green, white and red Italian flags and Jossy and Albert were wearing their best suits. Bob had a gondolier's shirt on but, apart from that, had not gone bananas. Glenda was in her best dress.

The boys noticed that Opal, Shaz, Melanie and Tracey had pushed right to the front of the crowd.

'Here. They're really strutting their stuff, aren't they?' said Ross. Ricky nodded. The girls were looking tip-top. Tracey was even wearing a dress and Melanie looked as though she had bought out the Max Factor counter.

Jossy was bellowing out last minute instructions on behaviour. 'Now, remember you lot, these Latin lads are our guests. I want no aggro. Lay off the smart aleck cracks. There will be no jokes about spaghetti, the Venus de Milo, or the World Cup – even though we did get further than them.'

A coach pulled slowly into the square. Not knowing any other Italian songs, Jossy, Bob and a couple of others burst into 'O Sole Mio'.

From the front seat of the coach a tall handsome

man waved and so did a couple of lads. Melanie, Opal and Shaz elbowed their way forward.

'Oh, some of them are dead fit,' Shaz was revealing some unexpected enthusiasms.

'Look, that one's got an earring,' Opal yelled as though she'd never seen such a thing before.

'Bags me the dishy, dark curly haired one with the beauty spot. But him in the yellow T-shirt's a belter too,' Melanie was gurgling.

These remarks did not go unnoticed by involved parties amongst the Giants. Ross turned to Tracey to comment but found that she was in the advance party too, weighing up the talent.

'I reckon the first "salvoes" in the war have been fired,' said Albert philosophically.

Jossy looked at him as though he had gone daft. He too edged forward as the tall Italian got off the bus and looked around.

'Mr Vito Cellini?' asked Jossy.

'You must be Jossy. El Capo.'

Jossy shook hands as Glenda bustled up beside him.

'This is my fiancée, Glenda Fletcher . . .'

Jossy got no further. Vito hurled his arms around Glenda and kissed her on both cheeks. Jossy blushed.

'You have exquisite taste in women, Jossy,' said Vito. This time Glenda blushed.

'I hope none of them lads tries to kiss me,' Ross pouted. 'I'll gob 'em.'

'I think they've got other targets than you in mind, Ross.' Glenda pointed to the girls who were giving the glad eye as the Italian lads got off the coach.

Ricky, Harvey, Glenn and Selly had pushed forward. They were able to hear the start of the chat.

Shaz buttonholed a big lad. 'I am Shaz.'

'I Nello, I striker,' said the lad.

'You'll do for me.' Shaz grabbed the Italian and his case. She began dragging him, through the crowd. Ricky pursued them.

'Hey, what about me? What about us?'

Shaz sneered. 'Oh, go and stick your head in a general knowledge book. You're so boring!'

The same sudden fate befell Harvey, Glenn and Selly. Opal and Melanie were like kids at a Pick 'n' Mix sweet counter. They grabbed and ran.

Jossy left the throng with a tall blond lad. He called Tracey over.

'This is Peppe. He's the skipper. I know you'll look after him, Trace.'

'Hi Trace,' said the lad.

'Tracey,' she blushed as she said it.

'Beautiful,' sighed Peppe.

Ross saw a real dozy look come over Tracey's face. It hurt. He came over and glared at Peppe. Jossy took Tracey to one side.

'Look, love. I know these lads are here to play football. But that doesn't mean they can't let their hair down a bit.' Tracey knew Jossy was trying to work a flanker because he would not look her straight in the eye. Jossy flannelled on. 'A few late nights won't do them any harm. Show them a good time. Get out on the razz.'

Ricky and Ross had been ear-wigging. Tracey moved off with Peppe.

'They've pinched our women, Boss.' Ricky spoke with a lump in his throat.

'Don't fret,' Jossy looked very crafty. 'Those lads are red-blooded – just like us. I reckon if they're tempted, those lads will fall.'

He turned back to see Glenda nodding and grinning at every word Vito came out with.

Within twenty-four hours of their arrival in Glipton, some of the Salvos were having to survive culture shock, as well as the hostility of the thwarted Romeos.

Shaz and Opal had decided to show their guests the finer points of making chip butties. They stood outside the chippy with breadcakes and hot chips at the ready.

'Hold this.' Shaz put half a breadcake in each of Nello's hands. Then she carefully placed a dozen chips across one half.

'Chip butty,' she enthused. 'Delicious!'

Nello took a bite but managed to squeeze half the chips onto the pavement. Shaz, Opal and Gianni fell about laughing.

The group did not notice Ricky and Harvey creeping up on them. Both grabbed a handful of chips from the newspaper that Opal was holding. They ran off chortling.

Shaz put a finger to her head and twiddled it round. 'Crazy boys.'

'Stupido,' added Opal.

The Italian lads shrugged.

Melanie's charms had captivated two of the Salvos. Now they were vying to buy her the ice-cream of her choice. Glenn and Selly were in hiding behind the ice-cream van.

'Would you like pistachio?' Paulo was being very charming.

'You lika da pistachio, Engleesh girl?' Glenn's voice echoed out but did not put the Italians off their stroke.

'Would you like chocolate mint chip?' asked Eduardo.

'I prefer greasy potato chip – 'cos I'm a big girl,' was Selly's contribution to the joke.

'Vanilla, please.' Melanie's voice was very firm. The Italians bought her two cornets as Glenn and Selly broke into song.

71

'Just one cornetto, give it to me . . .'

Glenn and Selly got two – on their heads. Melanie wiped her hands and gloated. 'I knew you were a pair of losers. But I must admit, you keep your cool!'

By 9.30 the next night the canal bank at Glipton was witness to a unique scene. Tracey Gaunt had gone overboard for the first time. She gazed up into Peppe's eyes as he talked about his home, his parents and his friends.

'Tracey. You have many friends-boys?'

She laughed at the phrase. 'Boyfriends? No.'

'Not some of the Giants? Some of them must be nice.'

'Oh, the lads are OK.' Tracey thought of Ross. 'But they think of me as one of the gang.'

'Gang!' Peppe laughed. 'You mean like in Al Capone movie? Shoot people?'

'No,' said Tracey and she laughed at his joke.

A few yards further along the towpath Peppe stopped and looked at his watch. 'I know it's a lovely night, carissima,' Peppe stroked her hair, 'but I have to go now to see Signor Vito.'

'But it's late. It's half past nine.' There was hurt in Tracey's voice.

'It is very important matter. About the team. I'll be back at your home in one hour. Ciao.' Peppe jogged off towards town. Tracey shook her head and sighed.

The next morning Magpie Sports was a hive of activity. Albert was doing his best to keep business going as normal but Bob and Jossy were agog over plans for that night's grand Italian Festival in honour of the Salvos. Bob had even drawn up a floor plan of the room and was putting crosses where Tracey and Co. would be acting as waitresses.

'I've planned it all like a military operation, Jossy. Those Italian kids will have a night to remember.' Bob was buzzing.

Jossy looked crafty. 'Now we want plenty of grub and drink for our guests.'

'No sweat,' said Bob. 'My mate Ted has let me have carafes of vino on the cheap – and there'll be endless fizz for the kids.'

'Great,' leered Jossy. 'We all know what appetites growing Italian lads have . . .'

'. . . especially before a big match.' Bob winked.

'So pile on the pasta . . .'

'. . . and the sauce.' Bob was loving it all.

'You'll make those Italians burst the way you're going on,' chided Albert.

'Geddaway,' chuckled Jossy.

The door clanged and Glenn and Selly mooched in looking very down in the mouth. They did not even bother to have a look in the full-length mirror. Jossy realized there was trouble.

'It's not fair, Boss,' said Glenn. 'The Italians have really stirred things up.'

'How?' asked Jossy sympathetically.

'They've pinched all our girlfriends. And they're rubbing it in. Everywhere you go in Glipton they're stomping around, blowing kisses. It makes you sick!' Selly glowered.

Before Jossy could say his piece, Harvey and Ricky came in.

'Those smarmy Italians had better watch it, Boss. I'm not usually a fighting man but they've really got my dander up.' Ricky was strutting like a fighting cock.

'It's definitely out of order, Boss. They've abused the spirit of friendship . . .' Harvey was cut off by Jossy's sarcastic laugh.

'Oh, the Italians have put your noses out of joint,

have they?' Jossy walked along the line of lads, looking each one hard in the eye. 'Well, let me tell you that the green-eyed monster, jealousy, is an evil thing. What you lot don't know is that I told Tracey and the girls to "entertain" them lads. So, what with courting, canoodling and late nights, their eyeballs will be hanging out on the pitch tomorrow afternoon. And tonight, at the "do", me and Bob are going to fill them choc-a-bloc full of pasta!'

'Charming,' breathed Albert.

Jossy cut him with a glance. 'All's fair, Albert, in love and football. So stop the moaning.'

The lads perked up a bit after this explanation of strategy.

'Right,' said Jossy, 'I'm off to Glenda's house for lunch with her and Vito. He'll never guess what we're cooking up for his lads, eh, Bob?'

'You are a case, Jossy Blair. You never miss a trick.' Bob winked at the others.

'You can say that again, Bob. I'll be back in an hour, Albert.' Jossy breezed out.

Half way down Glipton Town Street, Jossy eased his rapid pace to a saunter. The sun was shining, business was booming, the lads were working up a good burst of adrenalin for the match and he was on his way to see the girl of his dreams. He thought of how Glenda would look in her wedding dress; dark, sleek hair, a shy twinkle in her eyes, a slight flush . . . He had taken her out looking at furniture a couple of times. He had been surprised to find himself not only interested in settees and bathroom furniture, but positively enjoying it. 'You're a changed man, bonny lad,' he thought. On impulse Jossy detoured into the florists and bought £1.35's worth of freesias. He was considering a further detour to the betting shop just to weigh up the form when he bumped into Tracey. She was standing impatiently by an old horse trough that was something of a local landmark.

'Waiting for your horse to come to water?' quipped Jossy. He noticed that Tracey was not her usual perky self. 'What's up? Waiting for one of the lads? Or the girls?' Jossy twigged. 'You're waiting for the captain of the Italians. The big lad – Peppe.'

Tracey looked down and nodded. 'I've been waiting twenty minutes.'

Jossy tried to cheer her up. 'Look, he's probably training. Give him ten minutes then clear off. You'll see him at the "do" tonight.'

Tracey made an effort to cheer up. 'Going courting?' She smiled at the flowers.

'Summat like that.' Jossy gave her a broad wink and continued on his way. Whistling happily, he jogged the last quarter of a mile to Glenda's house. He let himself in and paused in the hall to check his hair in the mirror. A wave of Italian music came from the living room, then a sudden burst of male and female laughter. Jossy frowned.

'Ooh, you've got me all hot and bothered now.' Glenda's voice was very animated.

'But it's fun, is it not Glenda?' Vito's voice was full of fun – and charm.

Jossy's blood began to pound. This was definitely out of order. Carrying on behind his back! He flung the freesias into the brolly rack and stormed into the room.

Glenda and Vito was sitting together on the settee, the remains of a salad lunch in front of them and Jossy's plate untouched. They were huddled forward over the coffee table playing blow football. They both looked at Jossy's red face and giggled. Glenda blew Vito's hair askew with her blower.

'I hope I'm not interrupting anything private!' Jossy tried to sound sarcastic but failed.

75

Glenda straightened her hair. 'I had to entertain our guest, Jossy. You were late.'

Vito grinned. 'And you ask for all you get, my friend Jossy. You leave your beautiful fiancée with a full blooded Italian. What else can he do but play blow football with her?'

Glenda and Vito could not stop laughing. Jossy felt like an idiot but did not know what to say. Vito broke the deadlock.

'I must go now. I must buy some presents to take home. Are your boys training hard, Jossy?'

'Fine, pal. We're going to knock spots off your lot.' Jossy had not quite simmered down.

'Spots!' Vito exclaimed. Glenda tried hard to stop herself laughing out loud at Jossy's discomfort and his anger.

'It's a local phrase for a sound beating,' said Glenda.

Vito stood up, bowed politely to Glenda and made for the door. 'You seem confident, Jossy. I too have confidence. My boys are good.'

Jossy's face was no longer flushed. He was now, in fact, starting to feel a bit ashamed of his conduct. Vito stopped at the door and turned.

'May the best team win. Ciao, Glenda. Ciao, Jossy.'

'Ciao, Vito,' murmured Glenda, still chuckling.

'Tarra,' muttered Jossy.

Vito left and Jossy sat down on the settee a good few feet away from Glenda. She looked at him the way Miss Purdie, his teacher at junior school, had looked when Jossy had been shopped for pinching some apples from the vicar's orchard.

'What a way to treat a guest!' Jossy looked away sheepishly. 'That was jealousy – professional jealousy.'

Jossy twisted and gnawed his lower lip. 'You're wrong, pet, that was amateur jealousy.'

Glenda laughed and narrowed the gap between them.

EIGHT

Bob Nelson had really come into his own as architect-in-chief of the Glipton Giants' Grand Italian Night. It was open to dispute if he had Italian blood, as he claimed, but the gym was certainly a riotous display of colour. One of Bob's pals let him have a job lot of red and white check table cloths and another had stumped up some red candles. The latter glimmered on a couple of dozen tables. Small Italian flags and Union Jacks flew by the bread-sticks.

Tracey and the girls were run off their feet serving the food and drink. They looked very smart in red blouses and black skirts. Jossy had drawn the line at Bob's suggestion that the girls wear red roses in their hair. 'That's a bit wholesale, Bob. Let's not turn this do into a pantomime,' was his comment. Bob, Jossy and Albert were all wearing red gondolier's shirts with puffed sleeves. They too went among the tables seeing to every need of the Giants and the Salvos. Jossy was taking soup plates away from the table where Harvey, Glenn and Selly were sitting.

'You should have a fiddle and give us some serenading, Jossy.' Harvey had managed to get quite a lot of the minestrone on his chin and nose-end.

'There's enough fiddling going to go off later to please Yehudi Menuhin, kidda.' Jossy winked at them.

'Hurry up with the next course, Boss, I'm famished,' shouted Selly, as Jossy went to the kitchen.

Opal shot past Harvey's table with a tray full of pop for the Italians. Harvey tried to stop her but she dodged him. She was all google-eyed as she served the drinks to Nello, Eduardo and Gianni.

'Look at that,' hissed Glenn. 'Not only are we frozen out, but we could die of thirst for all those girls care!'

A space had been left in the middle of the floor for dancing and, in the interval before Bob's special spaghetti was presented, a few couples got up to dance to Dean Martin's 'Greatest Italian Hits'. Tracey stared into Peppe's eyes as they jigged around and Glenda came out of the kitchen to do a slow foxtrot with Vito. Nello, Eduardo and Gianni got up from their table and moved towards the door with a wave to Peppe. Ross moved to Ricky's table.

'I think those three are up to no good. I'm going to follow them.' Ross seemed to be telling only half of what was on his mind. Ricky nodded. Ross left.

All the waiters and waitresses had gone into the kitchen for the high spot of the evening. Bob walked into the middle of the dance floor and called for hush. *'Scusi, Scusi. Attenzione!* The rest of you pin back your lugholes. As you all probably know, the Nelsons are a very talented family.' This was roundly jeered. 'And one speciality of ours is cooking. So I have created a special dish for your delectation tonight – Spaghetti Gliptoni.' He waved to his menials. 'Bring it in please.'

Jossy, Albert and the girls bore in great steaming dishes and bowls of salads as all the boys clapped and cheered. Jossy put down his dish at one of the Italian tables. Melanie was serving the boys.

'Pile it on good and thick. Let them line their ribs, pet,' Jossy whispered to Melanie. He raised his voice to the Italian lads. 'Buono appetito, lads. Multo nosho!' He twisted a fork in the spaghetti and ate some. *'Bellissimo!'*

Seeing that the waitresses were all helping the Italians, the Giants helped themselves. Jossy arrived at Harvey's table to find Glenn and Selly tucking into portions the size of Mount Vesuvius.

'This stuff is ace, Boss. Pity we've got no chips to go with it,' said Glenn.

'I could eat a scabby donkey, Boss. I've had no tea, thanks to this shindig.' Selly was using a dessert spoon to gobble up the spaghetti.

'Go easy, you two,' screamed Jossy. 'It's the opposition I want bloated, not you lot.'

The boys took little heed as Jossy went back to the kitchen. Bob sidled up to Ricky's table. Ricky was tucking into a reasonably sized portion.

'What's in this, Bob? It tastes smashing,' asked Ricky.

Bob's eyes glowed like a wizard explaining how he had discovered the elixir of life. 'Prawns, anchovies, cockles, garlic, Oxo cubes and black pudding.'

Ricky suddenly lost a large percentage of his appetite.

Jossy had just completed a survey of how the special spaghetti was going down with the Italians. 'You've played a blinder, Bob. They're scoffing it like manna from heaven.'

'*Prego*,' beamed Bob. 'As we say in Italy – no problem.'

Bob and Jossy met Albert by Vito's table. He too was tucking in heartily. 'This is superb, Bob,' Vito enthused. 'It will make my boys homesick.'

'Sick is the word,' muttered Albert. He looked over at the table where Glenn and Selly were still forking, twisting and guzzling. Albert shook his head. 'The best laid plans of mice and men . . .'

There were some doleful faces amongst the waitresses. The three Italian heart-throbs had not reappeared and Peppe had sloped off too.

'I wonder where the lads have got to?' said Melanie.

Opal was optimistic. 'Oh, probably off buying presents.'

'At this time of night?' Shaz was not amused.

Tracey joined them with a frown on her face. 'I don't know,' she sighed. 'He's like the Scarlet Pimpernel is Peppe. The minute my back's turned, he's off.'

The meal was now over and there were one or two well fed Salvos about. Glenn and Selly could hardly walk with all the spaghetti they had put away. Vito stood up and walked to the middle of the floor, holding a package. He held up his hands.

'My English friends! May I first say how well we have eaten tonight.' Jossy winked at Bob. Vito went on, 'I would now like to make a small presentation to my very good friend, Jossy Blair.' Jossy bounced out onto the floor. The boys applauded. 'I would like to present to Jossy and the Giants a Salvos' pennant.' Vito took it out of the package. 'In the colours of the mighty Juventus!'

The Italian lads clapped loudly but a silence came over the Giants. The pennant was in black and white stripes – the Giants' colours. Jossy fiddled inside his shirt. He pulled out a similar pennant, inscribed *Glipton Giants*. There was no need to say anything; Vito twigged. Bob shuffled up behind Jossy.

'We can't both play in black and white,' said Bob, under his breath.

'Ten out of ten, Bob. What do you recommend?' Jossy wore a sickly grin.

'You've got to do the gentlemanly thing.' Bob nudged Jossy in the ribs.

'I have decided,' Jossy croaked, 'I have decided that tomorrow the Giants will take the field in our change strip of all white.'

'All white?' The joke went off like a damp Roman candle.

Albert tapped Jossy on the shoulder. 'I hate to say this, maestro, but the change kit is mucky. Remember all the mud and grot when we used it against the Sparrowhawks?'

Jossy rose to the challenge. 'Tracey,' he called, 'can you and the lasses wash that kit tonight and have it ready for the match?'

'OK,' Tracey's voice was leaden. 'We might as well. We've nowt better to do tonight, have we girls?'

'You can say that again,' said Melanie. Shaz and Opal nodded their agreement. The girls began moving out.

Glen and Selly led the lads to the door. They were both clutching their stomachs and groaning. They had eaten more than the Italian lads, and were now suffering.

'You've cocked up my plans, you two,' yelled Jossy.

'I don't know where you two put all that spaghetti,' said Harvey. 'You'll play rubbish tomorrow.'

A red-faced Ross shot in the door, very excited. He gathered Glenn, Selly, Ricky and Harvey round.

'Here, wait till you hear this. I've been on the trail of our Italian friends . . .'

The day of the match against the Salvos dawned crisp, dry and bright. It was an eleven o'clock kick-off so Jossy and Albert were at St James's Park shortly after nine to get things organized. Albert marked the lines whilst Jossy placed out the corner flags. Glenda busied herself in the tea bar making packed lunches for the Salvos to take with them on their journey home. At 10.15 Albert and Jossy had a tea break.

'Pitch is looking smashing, isn't it, pet?' Jossy was full of beans, eager for the coming contest.

'Yes,' said Glenda, pointing out two mugs of tea. 'I only hope the game is played in the true spirit of international friendship. The girls seem to have

81

been quite smitten by one or two of our guests.'

'Could make things out there a bit lively,' commented Albert. 'I don't suppose you've got a potted meat sarnie going spare?'

Glenda obliged. She looked out of the window. 'I can't help wondering what it's like in Sorrento now. The light dappling all the white fishing cottages round the bay . . .'

'One thing at a time, pet. Let's get today's business out of the way before we start planning ahead.' Jossy sounded nervous.

Ten minutes later the Giants began arriving in the dressing room. Jossy and Albert were laying out the stockings on the benches.

'Tracey should be here soon with the strips,' said Jossy, looking at his watch.

Glenn and Selly rolled in looking much less trendy and much less sprightly than usual.

'Ooh, I hope you're not counting on me to skin them today, Boss,' Glenn clutched his stomach. 'That spaghetti of Bob's doesn't half fill you up.'

'I never got a wink of sleep,' groaned Selly.

'Well, let's hope a half dozen of them Italians feel as rough as you, sunshine.' Jossy looked worried. 'Ten minutes to go and no strips! Anyway, gather round – game plan.'

The lads crowded round the blackboard. Jossy scribbled. 'Now, as I've told you, the Italians have this defence with a sweeper. What's it called?'

'Cappucino?' suggested Harvey.

'They'll be hot and bubbling at the back, that's for sure, so I want no pussyfooting around.' Jossy scrawled arrows on the board. 'I want you – Glenn, Selly and Ricky – into them tackles like spit off a hot shovel.'

There were cries of enthusiasm from the lads.

Tracey's blonde head bobbed around the door. She

had a rather strained half-smile on her face. There were odd giggles from the girls accompanying her.

'It's not like you to be late, Tracey,' Jossy sounded very harsh. 'You're usually right on the ball for punctuality.'

Tracey edged into the room timidly holding the bag with the kit. She received one or two tough looks from the lads.

'I'm afraid there's been a slight hiccup, Jossy.' There was a strong note of apology in the voice and more giggles from Melanie and company.

'I don't like the sound of that, Miss. How do you mean, hiccup?' Jossy thought a joke was in the offing.

As the lads drew near her with unconcealed hostility, Tracey unzipped the bag and slowly drew out a shirt. It had a number nine on the back and was coloured a very obvious pink! The boys did a fair imitation of a peckish wolf pack. Melanie dipped in the bag and pulled out a pair of pink shorts.

'We got some of our red hockey bibs mixed in with the kit. I think it's pretty. According to *Just Seventeen*, pink's in this season.' Melanie was loving every minute of it. Ross and the others were not.

'These birds have done this deliberately,' Ross shouted. The lads growled their agreement.

'It's a plot to make us look sissies in front of their Latin lovers.' Harvey glared across the room at Opal.

'I wouldn't be seen dead in that gear!' Wayne seemed to sum up the feeling of the meeting.

It was Ross, sharp witted as usual, who broke the atmosphere. Flashing his teeth, he strutted over to Tracey and grabbed the pink number nine shirt from her hands.

'I say this, lads.' The Giants were all ears. 'Let's put on this fancy gear and . . .' he turned to face the girls, '. . . then we'll trot out there and show these dollies what their Romeos are really like.'

Ricky and the lads twigged that Ross was thinking way ahead of the game. They followed suit as Jossy and Albert watched in amazement.

Ricky thrust out his chin at Shaz. 'Why don't you clear off and blow a few kisses at the opposition?'

'Yeah, buy your gigolos one last cornetto before we slaughter them,' rapped Harvey.

Tracey was the last of the girls to leave. She looked directly at Ross. 'Play it straight, lads. It's only a game.'

Ross grinned and his gaze swept the Giants before he replied. 'All's fair in love and war, pet – and, of course, football.'

There were about a hundred spectators scattered around the pitch as the Giants and the Salvos ran out. Nello, Peppe, Eduardo and Gianni made a bee-line for the stands and began chatting up Tracey and the girls avidly. The girls lapped it up.

Vito, looking very smart in a dark wool overcoat, lined up with the rest of the Salvos in front of the grandstand. He called for Peppe and the lads to join him.

Peppe was full of himself. 'Now we show you and the Giants what we Italian men are like. OK?'

Tracey smiled her smitten smile. *'A pui tardi.'* The Italians ran off.

The swelling strings and brass of 'Come Back to Sorrento' burst forth over St James's Park. Albert looked up from the cassette player to Jossy with a shrug. 'It's the best I can do. I couldn't find a copy of their national anthem.' Jossy nodded and stood to attention. After about a minute Albert changed the tape to 'Land of Hope and Glory' and the Giants, standing in line facing their opposite numbers, thrust out their chests and gave the evil eye to the Italians.

Nello tugged at Glenn's pink strip and a couple of the Italians giggled. At the end of the line, Vito grinned at Jossy.

'Everything coming up roses I see, Jossy.'

'Don't judge a book by looking at the cover, amigo.' Jossy was relishing the touch of aggro. He spoke loudly. 'Right, Giants, before the start of this historic encounter, I want you all to shake hands with our Italian friends.'

There followed what looked like an arm wrestling contest and there were plenty of verbal insults to go with it.

'You're on a hiding to nothing, son,' snarled Ross at the centre forward.

Ricky glared at Peppe as he offered his hand. 'We'll skin you, lover boy.' Peppe squeezed hard and Ricky winced.

Harvey danced about like a boxer waiting for the ball. 'You're in for a right licking,' he boasted to Gianni, who merely sneered.

As the music stopped, Ricky moved alongside Nello. 'I may look like a big soft nelly but at least it's not my name.' Nello thumbed his nose.

The referee called on the captains to toss up as Glenda joined Jossy and Albert in the stand. A few yards away Melanie was leading the cheers of the girls. 'Come on the Salvos!'

Glenda frowned. 'That's a bit out of order, Melanie.'

'Funny what love can do, pet,' cracked Jossy.

Glenda looked around. 'I wonder where Bob's got to. It's not like him to keep a low profile on the big occasion.'

'No, not like him at all,' said Jossy archly. Albert chuckled.

'What are you two plotting?' Glenda prodded Jossy's chest.

'Nothing, dearest. Now simmer down and watch the game. Attack the ball, lads!' Jossy was off and running.

With five minutes to go to half-time, the match was evenly balanced. The Giants' attack had been on song but the Salvos' defence, with Peppe a real powerhouse, had held tight. Now Peppe was pounding forward into the Giants' half. Wayne's tackle failed, then Glenn went flying off Peppe's shoulder. Peppe hammered the ball hard and Harvey, surprised by the sudden shot, missed it. 1–0 to the Salvos. Melanie and her backing group went spare.

'Bit physical that, wasn't it?' Jossy glared at Vito.

'Shoulder to shoulder. A fair charge,' came the reply.

Selly booted a hopeful through ball for Ricky to run onto. He collided with Nello. Both boys got up bristling.

'Fifty-fifty ball,' said Vito before Jossy could open his mouth.

Seeing Ricky about to grab Nello, Jossy yelled out: 'Steady Rick. Cool it. Get that goal back!' Ricky turned and began bawling at the lads.

As the seconds ticked down to half-time, Peppe raced into the area. Ricky timed his tackle perfectly. The ball skidded away but Peppe took off like an Olympic springboard champion. The whistle shrilled and the referee pointed to the penalty spot.

'What a con,' yelled Ricky. 'He took off when I was a couple of yards away.'

The protests did no good. Nello confidently slotted the ball along the ground past Harvey. The whistle blew for half-time. The Salvos beamed. Shaz and Opal hugged each other. Even Tracey looked pleased.

Jossy joined the Giants who were flopped out and sucking oranges.

'I don't know about having a sweeper – they're doing a hoover job on us, Boss.' Ross shook his head.

'Look, you're having no luck at all.' Jossy kept glancing towards the gate. 'Just keep at it, lads. The wind might soon be going out of their sails.'

'Where's my dad?' asked Ross.

'On the ball, son, that's where.' Jossy winked and suddenly Ross smiled.

'On the ball, yeah,' murmured Ross.

Bob's Mercedes swept through the gates, horn blaring. Everyone watched its progress to the grandstand. Bob leapt out and opened the passenger doors with a flourish. With wild shrieks four girls hurtled out and across the field to the Salvos. They were wearing the green school uniform and straw hats of 'Miss Chomper's Academy for Genteel Young Ladies'. Their conduct was not as genteel as Miss C. would have expected. They pounced on Peppe, Nello, Eduardo and Gianni like a posse of pop fans catching Duran Duran unawares. Vito tried to shoo them off but the clinches were unbreakable.

Ross ambled over to where Tracey and the girls were standing, frozen-faced.

'Who are they?' asked Tracey through her teeth.

Ross enjoyed every word. 'Well, if I was sitting where you four are sitting, I'd say they were the opposition.'

'You mean . . .?' Melanie was beetroot.

'A pew tardee,' drawled Ross.

'See you later,' hissed Shaz.

'Always slipping off at funny times.' Tracey shook her head.

Ross nodded. 'Yeah.' Ross was loving it. 'You shouldn't have been fooled by all that charm and chat, love.'

'It's better than we normally get round here,' shot back Tracey.

'That can be altered, chuck.' Ross began trotting back onto the field.

'Turn it on a bit, just for us, Ross.' There was a note of pleading in Tracey's voice.

'I'll do my best,' said Ross, not turning round.

'And, hey, Ross,' shouted Tracey.

'What?' he turned.

'Pink doesn't half suit you!'

The appearance of the rival girlfriends certainly knocked some of the stuffing out of the Salvos. Peppe in particular went to pieces and the Giants went to town. Two combined moves by Glenn and Selly sent Ross through to make the score 2–2. Ross could not resist a dig as he trotted past Peppe after the second goal.

'You shouldn't go round two-timing, pal. It takes all your strength away.'

Peppe did not understand but took it to be an insult because he made it his business to mark Ross from then on. Ricky played a long high ball into the Salvos' half. Peppe tried to get to it before Ross, and Ross did a perfect swallow dive over his outstretched foot.

'Crippled for life, ref. Get me to intensive care!' Ross twisted on the ground and the Giants crowded around protesting. Peppe howled his innocence but the referee pointed to the touchline. 'Off, son, professional foul.'

The Salvos were not pleased but Peppe trudged off with a wry glance at Tracey. He stopped near Vito and Jossy.

'Looked like our man dived, son,' admitted Jossy.

Vito nodded gravely. 'Looked like that to me, too.'

On the field the Salvos were at sixes and sevens. Ross took advantage. He dummied through the defence and lobbed the ball over the keeper. The Giants mobbed him.

'3–2 to us,' said Glenda to Vito. 'I'm afraid your pride will have to suffer today, Vito.' Neither Vito nor Peppe said a word.

Ross was leaping with delight. He hugged Ricky. 'See me take that dive before, lovely, wasn't it? I should have been in the Olympics. Poised on the board . . .'

The referee was standing just behind Ross. He heard every word.

'That's the worst piece of ungentlemanly conduct and unsporting play I've ever come across in fifteen years of refereeing. You, Nelson, are a disgrace. I'm bringing that lad back on!'

Pandemonium broke out as Peppe ran back into position. The Giants threatened all sorts of violence to Ross; the Salvos cheered; and Tracey, Melanie and company began supporting the Giants as never before.

Jossy and Vito shook hands with a grin.

The last minutes of the game saw the Salvos attacking like crazy. Ross even joined the lads in defence. But, carried away by the heat of the action, he forgot that he was five feet nothing and called 'mine' to Harvey as a centre came in. It cleared his head by six inches and sailed into the net. 3–3 was the final score.

There were one or two very sarcastic looks from various Giants in the direction of Tracey, Melanie, Shaz and Opal as the lads left the field.

Glenda turned from watching the girls' faces to where Jossy and Vito were nattering like old mates. 'Jealousy was never good to anybody, was it, Jossy dear?'

'No, pet, I think a few lessons have been learned in the past few days.' He sounded slightly sheepish.

Vito lifted the mood. 'Glenda, you and Jossy must come to Sorrento for your honeymoon.'

'Oh, yes,' Glenda's eyes sparkled. 'I can just see the moonlight on the water, the fishing boats. I can smell the blossom . . .'

Jossy cut in. 'I'm not so sure. That Italian television. No "Sportsnight". No "Match of the Day".'

'Absolute bliss,' sighed Glenda.

NINE

The visit of the Sorrento Salvos was still sending shock waves round Glipton three days after the match. Tracey really wanted to talk to Ross about things but she was too proud to approach him. Melanie blazed with fury at being conned but she would not show this in public so she retired to her bedroom to listen to her 'Great Years of Punk' albums. Opal saw Harvey at the ice rink and avoided him. Shaz had been really shaken. She tried waiting at the corner of Ricky's street but whenever he saw her he shot off in the opposite direction.

The Giants were not exactly raring to get back onto the football pitch. There was an air of anti-climax and general lack of motivation as they gathered at the Community Centre for training. One or two of the lads had evidence, too, of being in the wars.

Jossy and Albert were like two generals as they surveyed their pale and groaning troops.

'You'd think you lot had tried to pinch honey from the Chicago Bears,' Jossy sneered at them. 'I mean, I know them Italian lads were a little bit physical . . .'

'You might say that,' said Wayne dryly, his right arm in a sling. 'I got this just shaking hands with them before the kick-off.'

'What a bunch of softies,' mumbled Albert.

Glenn and Selly limped in, followed by a very down-cast Ricky. He looked awful.

'I hope you've not planned any tough training, Boss.' Ricky yawned. 'I'm cheesed off with football. Me life's getting too complicated to fit it in.'

Jossy leaned forward to have a closer look at him. 'You've been out on the tiles, haven't you? Your eyes look like pickled cabbage.'

'No, Boss. I lie awake at night thinking of schemes to avoid Shaz. She keeps hanging round waiting for me. And I don't think I want to see her – yet.'

'What happened to house hunting and mortgage enquiries?' Jossy's voice was thick with sarcasm.

'Give us a break, Boss. We've all had woman trouble.' Ricky's remark raised a rumble of agreement.

'Women,' Jossy was yelling now. 'I'm fed up of them sticking their noses in everywhere. This club is going to the dogs fast thanks to women!'

The door banged open and Ross staggered in, sporting a black eye. 'Every bone in my body aches, Boss. That match did my modelling career no good at all.'

Before Jossy could comment, Harvey came in, head deep in a horoscope magazine. He was reading out loud. 'The person at the centre of your emotional dilemma – emotional what?'

'Heart trouble,' translated Ricky.

Harvey read on. 'She is both attracted and yet repelled by your amorous intentions. What's it all about, Boss?'

'It means forget about women and concentrate on football – all of you.' Jossy threw Harvey's magazine away. Bob caught it as he came in. He glanced at it and grinned.

'Am I right in thinking that I have entered an environment lacking in willpower, drive and motivation?'

'Spot on, kidda,' sighed Jossy.

Bob pinged his braces and assumed his most self-satisfied manner. He went on walkabout. 'In my line of business – betting, import, export, wheeling and dealing – I have had more opportunity than most to observe what makes people tick. So I have been study-ing for a few months now the science of hypnotism.'

'Pull the other one, Bob,' growled Albert.

'Titter if you like, but I'm deadly serious.' Bob stopped in front of Harvey. 'We have here a highly sensitive lad who at times is a great goalkeeper but at other times dives about like a div. For various reasons he is not concentrating on his soccer prowess, so I will put him in a trance to bring out his true talents!'

The lads crowded round as Bob took off his med-allion and began to swing it in front of Harvey. In no time Harvey's eyes went glazed.

'I want your mind to go blank.' Harvey seemed to do this without any bother at all. 'Now, you are an orang-utang, king of your patch of the jungle. Show us your style!'

Harvey dropped to all fours and stuck his chin out. He began beating his chest and grunting.

'That's all we need between the goal-posts,' said Ricky.

'He'll be wanting nuts at half-time,' said Jossy.

As Harvey pranced around the shop, Bob pleaded with Jossy. 'Oh, come on, let's have a go at the rest of them, Jossy. They'd be putty in my hands. Under the trance they'd be as predictable as robots. They'd do whatever you told them.'

'No, Bob, I couldn't risk it. We'll have to find a different way to lift them out of this lethargy.'

'Look.' Bob was nothing if not a trier. 'I could give them all a key word like – final! Harvey – this is your final lap!'

Harvey gave one more shriek then returned to nor-mal. Bob winked at Jossy. 'We'll soon be in the final.'

Harvey dropped to all fours again. Jossy frowned at Bob.

'OK. That's final!' Bob spoke and Harvey stood up.

'You'd never send me over with hypnotism, Bob, my willpower's too strong,' crowed Harvey.

Jossy had been looking at a poster of Lester Piggot shooting past the winning post. 'What we need is something to get your juices jangling, make you eager for the fray.'

Albert raised his eyes to the roof. 'Not a day out at York Races studying the form!'

'There was no need for that, Albert. That's truly cutting. I'm hurt.' Jossy winked at the lads. 'No, I've got a super wheeze.'

'What is it, Boss?' asked Ricky.

'Surprise. Just you lot come along here tomorrow night at six and – er – bring the little women if you can.'

Jossy's 'wheeze' was in full flow the next night. It was, in fact, 'The Glipton Indoor Olympics' and featured pool, table football, shove ha'penny and table skittles. The girls twiddled and cued with great enthusiasm but the lads, apart from little Daz, were hardly putting their backs into the games. And there were a few nods and winks behind the backs of Albert and Jossy as they did the rounds.

Jossy passed by the pool table as Melanie played a crafty shot. 'Great stuff, pet. You've landed them right in the Branston Pickle there. That's a lovely snooker.' Harvey and Ricky did not look too worried.

At the table football Jossy edged aside Shaz and took the handles. 'The key to this game is wrists of steel and reflexes like lightning. Observe.' Jossy twiddled madly and cannoned the ball off the side wall. It trickled back towards his own goal. Shaz pushed him out of the way and resumed the game.

Shove ha'penny had always been Albert's game. 'Stroke the coins, Lisa,' he advised. Billy, who was her opponent, yawned loudly. 'Keeping you up, are we?' asked Albert, pointedly.

Albert joined Jossy by the table skittles board. Glenn was about to swing the ball when Ross whispered to him. 'Gee it up a bit, son, or they'll get suspicious.' Glenn crouched down, sighted carefully then swung the ball far too hard. It whizzed around, missing all nine skittles.

Jossy tut-tutted, shook his head and took hold of the ball. 'That's no way to approach this delicate skill, Glenn. Take heed. According to Hypotenuse, the ball should be directed on a balanced arc – thus – out of the back of the hand.' The ball swung lazily up and then dropped into the headpin. All nine skittles went down.

'A strike!' yelled Jossy.

'A fluke,' said Ross.

'Reminiscent of Edmonds,' said Ricky.

'Phil?' asked Jossy.

'Noel,' came the reply.

With a triumphant grin, Jossy made tracks to the door. Albert followed.

'Get stuck in, lads,' Jossy pleaded. 'Me and Albert's off for a jar. Remember, taking part is more important than winning. As we used to say at Newcastle – see you in the final!'

Harvey's eyes goggled. He picked up a pool cue and began potting balls all over the place. He sent the black in off five cushions. But the other lads were too busy to notice.

Bob and Glenda were sitting in the pub having a natter and waiting for Jossy and Albert.

'I've got this mate in Scarborough who's just bought a hotel.' Bob had mates everywhere. 'He says any friends of mine who want to try a couple of days there can do so free now it's out of season. Market research, like. Might be just the job for your honeymoon.'

Glenda almost choked on her Cherry B. 'Thanks for the thought, Bob. But I'm going a sight further than Scarborough for my honeymoon!'

The words were still echoing in the air as Jossy and Albert slipped in.

'Well, the girls are entering the spirit of things down the shop but I don't know about the lads,' Jossy moaned. 'Get the drinks in, Albert.'

As Jossy flopped down on the bench, Glenda leaned forward. 'I wonder if you've latched on to a convenient date for our nuptials, Jossy dear?'

'Nuptials. I've given them up, pet. I'm back on Puffed Wheat.' Jossy's joke amused himself and Bob but it did not do a lot for Glenda. She turned away in a huff.

Jossy realized the situation was delicate. He pulled his fixture booklet from his pocket. 'Seriously love, we're up to our eyes in games at the moment. There's the league and the cup qualifiers. Let's see . . .' He looked up suddenly. 'The lads worry me. There's no spark anymore. They lack any hint of the competitive spirit.'

In the shop, the 'Olympics' had taken on a new dimension and the boys were now participating with total enthusiasm. 'Place your bets, place your bets.' Ross's voice rang out. Noleen mopped his brow. Ross's hand was poised over a roulette wheel that was now in pride of place on the table football table. Des and Billy slid their chips onto the numbers. Their eyes gleamed with excitement. Ross's voice croaked in atrocious French: *'Rien ne va plus.'*

There was a similar scene being acted out on the pool table. Ricky was standing in front of a pile of ten and five penny pieces, breathing on a pair of dice. 'Come on old snake eyes, here we go!' He rolled the dice and held his breath. He had no luck that time but he and Shaz were back together. Shaz picked up the money. 'Never mind, love. This lot will go nicely towards buying our three-piece suite.'

Like a dove amongst hawks, Tracey moved quickly around the shop, too shocked to speak. She paused by the skittles table on which Harvey was now conducting a game of pontoon.

Even little Daz had been bitten by the gambling bug. He was playing pitch-and-toss on the shove ha'penny board. Glenn approached him, pulling out his empty pockets. 'I'm skint, Daz. Do you take American Express?'

'No,' came the reply. 'Neither do I accept pop bottle tops.' Daz flipped up his two coins and Tracey stepped in to catch them.

Daz saw from the look in her eyes that it was pointless to ask for his money back. Tracey left.

In the pub, Bob was still going on about his pal's hotel in Scarborough.

'Look, Jossy. You've got the lads going a bit with these games. Why not top it off with a few days at the seaside? Get them out on the beach, lungs full of fresh air.'

'Run them along the sand until their legs ache.' Albert spoke with relish.

'That's the idea, Albert. What do you say, Jossy?'

'Well. Let's just see if the games get them sparking. I admit the seaside would get them sound as a bobbin, but . . .'

Jossy was interrupted by Tracey who had sneaked

into the snug. The expression on her face did not bode well.

'Er – Jossy. I think you'd better come down the shop with me.' Tracey avoided their eyes.

'What's up, pet? They fallen asleep, sick of the games?' asked Jossy.

'Let's just say that the Glipton Olympics have lost a bit of the Greek idealism.'

Magpie Sports was still a den of iniquity when Jossy and Tracey walked in. They crept up to the dice game. Ricky still had the wild look in his eyes. He looked up, gasped when he saw Jossy, and tried to hide the dice. Without a word, Jossy scooped up the cash and gave it to Tracey.

Like avenging angels they moved on to the roulette. Jossy pulled at Ross's bow-tie and let it ping back on its elastic.

'*Rien ne va plus*. And I mean *plus*, kidda.' Jossy was white with fury. 'You'd better pray I don't tell your dad about this.'

Harvey was still holding the bank in the pontoon school. His back was to Jossy and he did not notice the looks on the faces of the kids opposite.

'Roll up, roll up,' shouted Harvey. 'Who fancies their chances against Maverick McGuinn?'

Jossy pulled the green eyeshade down over Harvey's mouth. He flung the cards all around the table.

'No need to throw a wobbly, Boss, it's only twopenny pontoon. Nobody was going to get skint.'

Jossy looked hard at Harvey. 'That's the way it starts, son. Twopences become tenners. Next thing you know, you owe some fat bookie two hundred quid!'

'You should know, Boss,' whispered Harvey.

Jossy scooped up the money on the table and handed

97

it to Tracey. 'See that Bob Geldof gets that pronto. Say Magpie Sports Aid raised it on a fun run.'

The lads looked thoroughly dejected and their lady friends were none too merry either. Tracey leaned near Jossy. 'The quicker you take up Bob's offer and get this lot to the seaside, the better.'

Jossy nodded his agreement. 'Yes, duck. At least in Scarborough we can keep tabs on them.' He cast a scornful look over the Giants. 'Go on home before I call the Vice Squad.'

TEN

There was a steady grey drizzle of rain as the Giants assembled in Glipton Market Place to board the coach for Scarborough. It matched the mood of their girl-friends. In a way, getting into trouble together at the 'Glipton Olympics' seemed to wash away all the jealousies roused by the Italian visit. Now there were one or two tear-stained faces and hushed voices as Jossy ushered the party on to the coach.

'All aboard. All aboard. Last kisses and cuddles now. You should have said your fond farewells last night.' Jossy grinned at Glenda and Tracey as they climbed on the coach.

'Give it a rest will you, you're strangling me!' Ross was wrestling off the attentions of Lisa and Noleen. 'I'll send you each a card and I'll bring you a stick of rock. Now can I have my arms back?'

Glenn and Selly paraded up with Melanie. Both lads were wearing sunglasses and carrying buckets and spades. Melanie carried their inflatable dinghy.

'Hi, Boss.' Glen was cock-a-hoop. 'Do you reckon we'll get some sun? I hear that the weather in Scarborough is very changeable.'

'This is not a jolly,' Jossy hissed. 'We're going to the seaside to tone up, not to swan about. The dinghy definitely stays here.'

Glenn and Selly got on the coach.

Shaz was now in a flood of tears and Ricky was doing his best to console her.

'Don't fret, precious,' Ricky looked round to check who might be earwigging, 'It's only for a couple of days.'

'Write to me twice a day. I want to share all your thoughts.' Shaz was really on song.

'I won't have time to have any thoughts, love,' Ricky turned to meet Jossy's beady eye. 'The Führer will have us training morning, noon and night.'

'Come on, Ricky. Give your old lady one last loving peck.' Jossy's voice was sarcastic. He added, under his breath, 'He'll never be off the phone to her.'

Harvey arrived with a blissful look on his face, due mainly to the fact that Opal was giving him more attention than ever before.

'You don't seem absolutely chuffed about this trip, Harvey,' Opal batted her eyes. 'Are you sad to be leaving me?'

'You what?' Harvey was definitely miles away.

'This is your final chance. Do you want a kiss or don't you?' Opal's tone was huffy.

Harvey changed in a flash. He beat his chest, took her in his arms, and gave her a great smacking kiss.

Opal was pleasantly shocked. 'Harvey, don't go chasing girls at the seaside.'

'See you soon, honeybunch.' Harvey bounced onto the coach.

Jossy waved at the driver to start.

After an hour of the journey Jossy leapt into action. He stood up in the front of the coach with a video in his hand.

'Right, you lot. This little exercise in motivation is about to start. I have here highlights of the 1986 World Cup. Remember Maradona waltzing past five England players to slot home? Remember all that wonderful shooting and dribbling? Well sit back, watch and absorb. Glenda, would you do the honours please?'

As Glenda took the video with a demure smile, Ross marched down the gangway holding a video of his own in his hand. He handed it to Glenda.

'I have been delegated by the lads to ask our Boss's permission for one last bit of fun before we buckle down to the hard slog ahead of us.' There was a chorus of encouragement as Ross went on. 'Please, Boss, can we have "Raiders of the Lost Ark"?'

Again Glenda smiled sweetly as she took the second tape. She moved forward to the video machine, pausing to take yet another video from her handbag.

'Gentlemen, as Tracey and I are your guests – I think it only right that we should choose the inflight movie.'

The lads groaned and pretended to be sick as the slushy music of 'Dream Romance' filled the coach and Tracey and Glenda made themselves comfortable.

'Take it off, Boss,' pleaded Ricky.

'You take it off, sunshine,' Jossy shut his eyes, 'or sit back and watch – you might pick up a few tips!'

Scarborough was one of Jossy's favourite places. He had been taken there on holiday a couple of times as a boy and once he had spent a training week there with Newcastle United. It would be great running along the beach in the mist with the lads; waking in the morning with the sun on the sea and the gulls shrieking, and in the evening taking a stroll along the fairy-lit promenade with Glenda. The lads' excited shouts woke Jossy. They were all clustered to the seaward side of the bus as it ran on to the foreshore. An enormous rainbow stood out against the rich blue sky. The sun lit up the castle and the amusement arcades.

'Can we go straight out for a look around?' begged Wayne.

It was just approaching twelve noon so Jossy mentally worked out a quick timetable.

'Right. We'll work ourselves into this gradually. After lunch you can all go your separate ways. But I want to see everybody at nine o'clock tonight in the hotel lobby.'

The lads cheered and Tracey and Glenda decided on a shopping expedition.

Half an hour later, Jossy and Albert finished booking everyone into the hotel. It was all going very smoothly until the receptionist pointed out a slight snag.

'I'm afraid there's only one room left now and it has only one double bed.' The girl looked from Jossy to Albert.

'You mean for us two?' Jossy thought it was a joke. 'Yes.'

'We'll have to kip together, old son. Come on.'

Albert and Jossy took the lift to their room. There was hardly space to swing a cat. Jossy sat on the bed.

'Here's us dossing together – and the lads living in the lap of luxury. Anyway, what do you fancy doing?'

'I thought I'd go and see my cousin. He goes fishing most days. Fancy coming?' asked Albert.

'No,' said Jossy. 'I might have a quiet pint and a game of dominoes. See you later.'

There was a spring in Jossy's step as he took the cliff lift down to the seafront. Though it was mid-October, there were still day trippers about – but no one was paddling. Several bingo and amusement arcades were doing good business. The good weather had even encouraged the donkey owners to start operations on the sands. Opposite the crab stalls Jossy turned into the Cod and Lobster.

There was the usual bunch of ruddy-faced fishermen, with tartan scarves knotted at their throats, lining the bar. Jossy edged through them and ordered a pint of bitter. As he took his first sip, he heard loud Geordie voices coming from the games room. He sidled up to the door and got the shock of his life. In the corner of the room Johnnie the Runner, trilby tilted back and cigar on the go, was shuffling the dominoes.

'Now don't shuffle the spots off these Yorkshire dobs,' joked a young blond lad sitting opposite Johnnie. Johnnie's eyes raised from the table and caught Jossy's.

'Well, look what the wind's blown in! We're not in Scarborough two hours and we bump into Jossy Blair!'

Jossy walked across the room to meet the other members of the Byker Jolly Boys.

'I'm here with my team, the Giants,' said Jossy. 'I'm toning them up – with any luck.'

'Well, an hour with your countrymen will do you no harm.' Johnnie made tracks to the bar. 'Where's that fiancée of yours?'

'Shopping,' said Jossy as he fondled the dominoes. Johnnie came back with a fresh round of drinks. 'Hey,' cried Jossy. 'Steady with the beer. I'm here in my capacity as Boss of the Glipton Giants.'

'A pint won't stretch your capacity,' Johnnie chuckled. 'Now shuffle.' Johnnie addressed himself to the rest of the party. 'This lad is a fine dobs player. I taught him myself!'

'So he'll cheat like an expert,' came the reply.

An hour later Jossy and the lads left the pub in fine fettle. The Jolly Boys had a scheme that lived up to their name. They fancied placing a few bets on a donkey race. Trade was not exactly brisk so the donkey lady was easily persuaded to let the Geordies take over for a little while. Two of the lads held the donkeys all together at one end of the course, whilst Jossy, Johnnie, and the rest stood at a finishing line marked out on the sand. Johnnie acted as the bookie and Jossy put fifty pence on Loppylugs. It came in a miserable fifth out of six runners.

The lads caught the donkeys and the second race started. Jossy went along with Loppylugs again and this time he encouraged him. 'Come on, Loppy, get going!' he yelled. Suddenly aware of an audience, he turned.

Ricky, Ross and Harvey had grins on their faces like Cheshire cats. Johnnie came over with a handful of money.

'You lost again, Jossy, but I'm doing fine. Fancy another fifty pence?'

'I've seen it all now. Putting money on donkeys!' Ricky shook his head.

'Just a joke, lads,' Jossy was twisting. 'This is Johnnie the Runner, an old pal of mine from Newcastle.'

'Ye lot must be the Giants.' He nodded at Jossy. 'Your manager never could back winners.'

Ricky nodded. 'He's brought us here to learn to discipline ourselves.'

Johnnie laughed. 'Don't do as he does, do as he says.'

The lads drifted off towards the town. Jossy said his farewells to Johnnie and the Byker Mafia and went back to the hotel. He lay on the bed for an hour, then played snooker by himself until it was time for dinner. He was getting poshed up when Albert came into their room.

'The lads are all downstairs ready to go in to dinner. They're all clean, smart and quiet. I can't think what's got into them.' Albert sounded shocked.

'It's this sea air,' said Jossy. 'It's got them tired, Albert.' Jossy assumed his tone of command. 'Go and tell the lads that I want them all in bed by nine because we're up with the larks and working hard tomorrow.'

'Aye, aye, sir,' said Albert and went off to obey orders.

At ten to nine that night Glenda was in seventh heaven. She and Jossy were strolling along the terraces of the Spa Gardens, bright fairy lights twinkling above them and the sea pounding the cliffs below. Glenda shook her hair in the wind and cuddled closer to Jossy.

'Oh, isn't this romantic, Jossy? Just us alone with the elements.'

'I certainly feel smashing, pet. That halibut I had was spot on. In fact I'll bet it was sporting just beyond the lighthouse this very morning.' Jossy was being jokey, but the atmosphere had got through to him too.

Glenda entered the frivolous mood. 'My steak au poivre was absolument parfait.'

'You should've sent it back then!'

Glenda thumped Jossy playfully. 'I knew you were going to say that.'

A young couple were approaching them, deep in conversation. Jossy recognized a familiar note in the laughter. He tugged Glenda under an overhanging tree.

'Ssh,' hissed Jossy.

Glenda gasped slightly when she realized that the couple were Ross and Tracey. After waiting a moment or two, Jossy led Glenda to the middle of the path.

'The love bug is well and truly out on the prowl tonight,' said Jossy, with a glance after Ross and Tracey.

'Yes, pet,' sighed Glenda, gripping Jossy's arm a fraction tighter. 'It bites everyone sooner or later.'

'I hope the rest of the lads are all right.' There was panic in Jossy's voice. He turned back towards the hotel. 'I think we'd better start back, love. I want to make sure the lads are in kip by nine.'

'But it's such a lovely night, Jossy.'

'It'll be a lovely tomorrow night as well, pet. And the way I'm going to put that lot through their paces, we can go for our walk at seven. They'll be shattered and horizontal by then!'

Albert was waiting for them in the hotel foyer, a worried look on his face. 'You're not going to like it, Jossy, not one little bit.'

'Problems, old son?'

Albert took an extra deep breath. 'I've been all round the rooms. The lads aren't in bed. They're not even indoors. We've lost them!'

Jossy raised his nose to the air like Scooby Doo. He took a couple of deep sniffs. 'I'd know that smell anywhere.' He pointed to a door leading off from the foyer. 'I'll bet my smeller takes us to the Giants.'

'You've lost me,' admitted Albert.

'Follow me, dear Watson.' Jossy led the way across the foyer. 'That smell, Albert . . .' He kept his nose in the air. 'That smell is fish, chips, faggots, mushy peas and, if I'm not mistaken, curry sauce!'

Jossy opened a door and led the way down a set of stairs. The sounds of 'A-ha' drifted upwards. They passed a sign saying *Leisure Oasis*.

'Obviously where Sheikh Rattle 'n' Roll hangs out,' muttered Albert as he and Jossy hid behind a rubber plant.

Their eyes fell upon a bizarre scene. The 'oasis' was a breeze block and plastic tribute to the Flintstones. Cave-like walls and jungle surrounded a jacuzzi, pool and several items of keep-fit apparatus. The Giants were draped all over the shop, digging in to pop and chips. Wayne, wearing a cardboard cowboy hat, sprawled amongst the bubbles of the jacuzzi. Harvey lazily pedalled an exercise bike, Walkman in his ears, straw in a can of Fanta. Glenn and Selly sat by the pool dipping chips in curry sauce, while Ricky sailed round in a dinghy.

But, if anything, what shocked Jossy and Albert

106

most was the sight of Tracey in this tableau of sloth. She and Ross were sitting at a table sharing a Knicker-bocker Glory.

Jossy rose from the plastic jungle like Tarzan accosting a bunch of ivory hunters. 'What a team!' The action froze. 'We haven't been in this place ten minutes and you've turned the aerobics annexe into a doss house.' He fixed his glare on Tracey. 'And as for you, I thought I could trust you.' Tracey dropped her head in shame.

Harvey, still plugged in to his own music, was pedalling away merrily, unaware of Jossy and Albert's entrance. Jossy strode over to him and removed the earphones.

'Hi, Boss. It's ace here. You don't half bring us to some belting places,' enthused Harvey.

Jossy walked to the door. He turned and looked at his watch. 'I want the lot of you out of here in two minutes flat. And — I want you all down on the beach at eight sharp. Before breakfast!'

ELEVEN

Scarborough beach had seen some strange sights over the years, everything from wooden bathing machines to shipwrecks, but rarely had such a motley crew paraded there as the Glipton Giants. Nobody seemed to have slept very well. There were yawns and bleary eyes all round. On the other hand, Jossy and Albert were bright-eyed and bushy-tailed. Jossy pulled a large, old-fashioned stone bottle from his holdall. His eyes gleamed as he removed the stopper and sniffed the contents.

'By, that's a drop of the real stuff.' Jossy's nose wrinkled.

'What is it, Boss?' asked Ricky innocently.

'You'll soon find out, kidda. It'll sort out the worst effects of chip poisoning! Get in a line.'

All eyes were on the bottle as the lads scrambled into position. Tracey, who had now rejoined the bosses, took a dessert spoon from her pocket. The gleam of mischief sparkled in Jossy's eyes.

'Right, my bonny lads. The buck starts here.' Jossy did a good Long John Silver impression as he shuffled along the line of boys. 'In olden days people used to flock to Scarborough to take the spa waters. They thought it would give them a boost. So, here goes. Open wide!'

He poured a trickle of a fluid that looked like weak

Tizer into the spoon that Tracey held under Ross's nose.

Ross slurped the mixture down and turned green. The others pleaded and postured but swallowed their share. Harvey protested most strongly but with Albert holding his nose and Jossy his jaw he took the medicine.

Jossy looked at their twisted faces. 'Any slacking in the next couple of hours and you get second helpings! Right?'

The next hour more than made up for all the high jinks. Under the orders of Jossy and Albert, the lads ran, jumped and strained like paratroopers. A breather was called for drinks.

'He isn't half getting his own back now,' sighed Ross.

'Live with it a little while longer.' Harvey sounded sly. 'Then follow me.'

Some of the lads exchanged puzzled glances. Harvey was acting like a master spy. Innocent-eyed, he walked around the flopped-out lads offering encouragement.

Tracey had had enough. 'Bye, lads. I'm off to keep Glenda company. See you back at the ranch – if you make it.' She winked at Ross, who blushed slightly.

'Right, on your feet.' Jossy was bouncing with enthusiasm and energy. 'We will round off today's proceedings with a three mile run . . .'

'But we're all shattered, Boss,' pleaded Wayne.

'No, we're not,' yelled Harvey. He was on his toes, bristling. 'We came here to get fit. Lead on, Boss.'

'What's got into him?' said Albert.

'Must be the spa water doing its bit,' said Jossy. 'To make life a bit more interesting, our run will be through some of the most scenic parts of Scarborough. OK. Let's go!'

Things went fine until Jossy led them all into a large

park with a boating lake. Jossy put in a spurt and came to a gasping halt near the edge of the lake.

'Right, lads, you've done well. We'll rest ten minutes then we'll jog back to the hotel.' He turned. The lads were nowhere to be seen. Nor was Albert!

At the hotel, Glenda and Tracey were having coffee in the sun lounge and chatting away like bosom pals.

'So everything will be planned down to the last crumb of wedding cake and every last metre of the honeymoon itinerary, dear.' Glenda sounded like a general bragging about a favourite battle. 'You, naturally, will be a bridesmaid – if you want to, of course.'

Tracey nodded eagerly. 'Oh, that's smashing. I've never been a bridesmaid before.' She paused and continued with a slight frown. 'I hope you don't mind me getting a bit personal – but I'd appreciate your advice on a certain matter.'

Glenda leaned forward, smiling like the good fairy in a pantomime. 'Spill it out, love.'

'I've had this letter from a lad, you see, and it's put me in a bit of a spot.' Tracey paused, then went on. 'He's called Rupert and he lives in the South. He wants me to go to London to see a hockey match and then go out with him. I was going to the match anyway but I'm not sure I want to see him.'

'Why not?' asked Glenda.

'Well, I still quite like Rupert – but I really fancy Ross now. I think he's less bigheaded. At least when he's away from the lads. What should I do?'

Glenda did not answer right off. She looked out of the large window at a green and white fishing boat curving out of the blue bay past the lighthouse. She sighed softly.

'Tracey dear. You'll learn that in life the heart is a

110

lonely punter. We take risks every day. Some of us are attracted to men like Ross and Jossy who are real scallywags.'

'You mean . . .' Tracey leaned forward.

'Give Rupert the elbow.' Glenda's eyes flashed like lights on a Christmas tree. 'In the nicest possible way, of course. More coffee?'

Harvey had led the 'great escape' and he and the lads were now heading for the amusement arcades on the seafront.

'Jossy deserves it.' Ross did not sound too sure. 'He pushed us to the limits of human endurance.'

The rest nodded and dispersed among the fruit machines.

'Ta-ra, lads. See you later.' Harvey sloped off. He jogged along the promenade and up a side street. He looked up at a sign that read 'Gipsy White Rose – Half Yorkshire – Half Romany'.

'It's a rum mixture,' thought Harvey and shot inside.

Gipsy White Rose sat in front of a purple curtain covered in gold stars. She lifted her shrewd eyes from her crystal ball and looked hard at Harvey. He noticed that there were dozens of rings on her fingers.

'If I cross her palm with silver, it'll look like a scrap-yard,' thought Harvey.

'Hey up, young feller, hast come to me for advice on brass – or affairs of the heart?' The voice rasped like sandpaper but it was still friendly.

'The heart actually. I've got this bird, you see, and I just can't work her out.' Harvey gave the gipsy a pound and went on to describe the up and down moods of Opal.

'Tha's picked a reet deep lass to be thy sweetheart.' The gipsy nodded gravely.

'Pardon!' Harvey was extra polite.

'I'm saying the lass is deep. She takes some working out, this Opal.'

'Yeah,' said Harvey. 'But does your glass ball say anything about her falling for me?'

'I'll have one final look . . .'

Harvey's eyes rolled at the word 'final'. He stood up and turned. He was out of the door in a flash.

'I allus said them Lancastrians were a queer bunch.' The gipsy sighed and gave her crystal ball a quick polish with a duster.

The lads had by now tired of the slot machines and were wandering aimlessly along the promenade. Wayne spied the San Francisco-type cable cars that ran up the cliff.

'Come on, that's for us!' he shouted. The Giants piled in and pushed their faces to the windows as the car began the ascent. A tracksuited figure jogging up the two hundred steps to the top looked up as the cable car passed. Jossy's eyes boggled. Most of the lads tried to hide but Glenn and Selly waved breezily. Jossy shook his fist at them. At the top the lads dispersed sharpish in all directions.

Gipsy White Rose was doing a roaring trade. Albert came out of the booth grinning all over his face. He was dying to tell Tracey the good news. And he did not have to wait long because round the corner came Glenda and the girl herself.

'Oh, Albert, fancy seeing you here,' gushed Glenda, 'I thought I'd have a bit of a giggle and visit the fortune teller.' With that she swept into the booth.

Albert was almost jumping up and down with excitement. 'She says Magpie Sports is going to go from strength to strength. She says she sees a dark-haired woman in a position of power . . .'

'Glenda on the board of directors,' said Tracey dryly.

Ten minutes later Glenda walked out of the booth looking like she had just won the pools.

'I can't believe it. I'm all goosey. Gipsy White Rose says she can see a beautiful bay surrounded by little white cottages. That must be Sorrento. And it must be my – er – our honeymoon. But I don't know where the big, black cone-shaped hills come in.'

'Coal tips, like they have in the North East?' Tracey grinned cheekily.

'Oh, I think not, dear,' said Glenda very seriously.

Albert, very diplomatically, said nothing.

'Let's go for a row on the boating lake,' suggested Tracey.

'Good idea,' said Albert and the trio set off.

Soon after their departure, a very tired Jossy Blair jogged to a halt outside Gipsy White Rose's premises. The lads had now disappeared completely and Jossy was getting a bit worried about them. In his betting days luck had always been an important factor in Jossy's selection of horses. He now looked at the gipsy sign and shrugged.

'What have I got to lose?' he said to himself and sidled into the booth.

'How art tha today, my lad?' rasped the gipsy, glad of all the business.

Jossy sat down and looked around warily. Gipsy White Rose bent forward and cupped the crystal ball in her hands.

'I see horses galloping across emerald turf . . .'

'That's my past, I want to know about the future,' said Jossy, sarcastically. Then he added more graciously, 'Look pet, I've lost a football team of little lads. Can you help me?'

The gipsy again wrapped her hands round the ball and gazed into its creamy depths.

'The picture I'm getting is cloudy and steamy . . .'

'They're not filling their bellies with chips again, I hope,' sighed Jossy.

'Wait. I see water. Boys, little boys – real scallywags. They are beside water.'

Jossy stood up and gave the gipsy a pound coin.

'I'll try the sea and the boating lake. They'll get into hot water when I catch up with them.'

Maybe it was the sight of the slate-grey North Sea that set Jossy off in pensive mood as he walked back to the hotel. He had fully expected the lads to be a bit of a handful at the seaside, but now he was really worried about them. In a couple of weeks' time he and Glenda would be married and they both wanted a family. His own sons would be as tearaway as the Giants. He grinned at the idea.

Suddenly the thought of actually getting married frightened him. Like a drowning man he surveyed the highlights of his past life. His Uncle Jimmy giving him his first tatty old leather football to kick round in the back lane. His first 'love affair', with Jennifer Hobson who had jilted him after a dizzy month and fallen for a waltzer cowboy off the funfair. His first England schoolboy cap. Then the fateful day at St James's Park when he broke his leg. Now the massive responsibilities of marriage loomed.

Jossy looked out over Scarborough Bay. A deep sea fog lurked over Filey Brig, a rocky outcrop to the south, and a harsh wind whipped the grey waves to white. But from the north a shaft of sunlight crept through the gloom and burst over the ruin of Scarborough Castle. Jossy perked up. At least teaming up with Glenda meant problems shared. He jogged towards the hotel, whistling vigorously.

Glenda was waiting for him in the foyer, the look of love and affection in her eyes. 'I've just been talking

114

to the boys, pet. They're ever so upset at doing a bunk.' She took him by the arm like a nurse with a stroppy patient. 'But Albert and I, with Tracey's help, have cooked up a scheme to get your own back on them.'

Jossy let her lead the way to a couple of deep plush armchairs in the lounge.

'Glenda,' his voice was strained. 'Do you think we should have two kids or three?'

Glenda flopped in the armchair, mouth agape.

'I mean, as the lads are proving, young kids are a real handful.'

'I'll have to think about this, Jossy.' Glenda composed herself as Albert and Tracey joined them.

'Sorry I dipped out on the jog, Jossy. But my lungs aren't what they used to be.' Albert was looking crafty. 'But wait till you hear what I've fixed for our disappearing little friends.'

The snooker room of the hotel was one of the last jewels of Victorian elegance in Scarborough. The walls were hung with tapestries and the coffee tables and chairs were carved in dark wood. The boys added a dash of modernity in their vivid tracksuits but their mood was sombre. Ricky idly cued up on an easy red. 'He's going to go absolutely stark raving crackers.' Ricky spaced out the words, hit the white and missed.

Wayne was playing with the pigtail that hung from his soul brother hairdo. 'Right on, man. We came here to train. Really motor . . .'

'And we blew it.' Ross crashed the white into a pack of reds. None went down.

Harvey, as usual, tried to look on the bright side. 'You never know. He might see our doing a runner as our need for mental relaxation. We'll go like greyhounds after this.'

Nobody was much convinced by the argument. The

115

door clicked and the lads froze. Jossy walked in, followed by Albert and Tracey. They carried full black plastic bags. Silently they trod the deep carpet. Jossy had an icy grin on his face.

'Oh, nice to see you chaps enjoying yourselves.' There were iron filings in the tone. 'Don't stop your game – I hope you're in the Steve Davis class soon – but hear this and hear it good.' The tone was now hot steel. 'You have turned this training trip into a farce at the expense of me and Albert here.' Albert nodded grimly. 'So the programme of events for tomorrow will more than make up for the jolly japes of today. I want you all on the coach at 06.00 hours.'

The lads gasped but said nothing.

'We have arranged a special little exercise session, thanks to Albert's old buddy from his army days, RSM Roberts.'

'But Albert was in the Catering Corps,' chipped in Glenn.

'We'll cater for you all right tomorrow,' quipped Jossy.

'That we will,' added Tracey.

Solemnly Jossy, Albert and Tracey emptied the bags. Out fell army camouflage overalls, hats and heavy boots. Albert started to whistle 'The British Grenadiers' at funereal pace.

It was like a scene from a movie about the French Revolution. Through an avenue in some tall pine trees moved the Giants, all blindfolded. Tracey and Jossy led the column and Albert brought up the rear, chanting 'left, left, left – right, left.' All the scene needed was a man with a balaclava standing by a guillotine.

'Halt!' yelled Albert, and the boys bumped into each other. 'Remove blindfolds.' The boys obeyed and their eyes stood out like organ stops as they surveyed the

116

assault course. It was like a jungle, made even more hostile by steel scaffolding, ropework and high brick walls. Jossy and Albert grinned hugely.

'They're sadists,' hissed Ross.

'You're right. We could cop a serious injury on this lot. I'm telling me mam,' said Ricky.

'I'm making my will,' said Harvey.

'Right lads.' Jossy was almost cooing with glee. 'Just imagine this lot is a funfair, or a boating lake, or an amusement arcade maybe. Run riot!'

In roughly twenty minutes flat, Jossy got his own back. Albert's pal, the RSM, had organized soldiers to be on hand to help the lads over the toughest parts of the course. All the boys did their best and Jossy, Albert and Tracey urged them on. One by one they staggered home and flopped down. Harvey was last.

'How about one final go over the wall, Harvey?'

Harvey reacted to his key word as if electrocuted. He shot off.

'We'll have to get Bob to undo the spell,' said Albert.

'Might come in useful at key times in big matches,' mused Jossy, half seriously.

On the bus the lads flopped around, groaning and puffing. After ten minutes of the journey back to Glipton, Jossy shouted out to them. 'Who's ready for "Raiders of the Lost Ark"?'

He got no reply except a small volley of snores. He exchanged smiles with Glenda.

TWELVE

The trouble with the Glipton Giants was that some of
the players were good footballers – and they knew it.
Glenn and Selly were very good dribblers, but did not
see why they should practise passing the ball. Wayne
was a lovely mover in midfield, but he was very lazy.
And Ross – well he was either a goal-hanger in the box
or a very selfish winger. It took Jossy to spot these
faults and get the team working.

A few days after their return from Scarborough, the
Giants were really putting their backs into training at
St James's Park. In a week's time there was a cup
match against arch-rivals, the Ecclestone Express, and
on the same Saturday it was Jossy and Glenda's wedding. Glenda did not know about the cup match, and
Jossy hoped and prayed that she would not find out –
until afterwards!

'Come on, lads. Drive yourselves,' Jossy yelled, as
Ricky and Ross led the run around the field. Shin-pads
were tossed aside now and the boys were red-faced
with effort.

'They're really grafting now, Jossy,' said Albert.

Glenda picked her dainty way over the turf to Jossy's
side. Jossy saw her coming through the corner of his
eye.

'Not a word about the cup match,' he whispered to
Albert. Albert winked his assent.

'Hello, dear,' Glenda gushed. 'I've just come to check

a few small details about arrangements for the wedding. First, cars. The ceremony is at two prompt. I'll be picked up at quarter to. Shall I book a car for you?'

Jossy had half an eye on the 5-a-side match that the lads had started. 'Leave my transport to me, pet,' he said, absently. 'Put some humpty into it lads!' He turned back to Glenda. 'It's no sweat, love. I'll fix my own wheels.' Then back to the Giants. 'Let's see some commitment in those tackles lads.'

'I hope you won't be cutting any corners, Jossy.' Glenda put on her little girl lost voice.

'Corners! I'll not be cutting, taking or thinking of any on Saturday, pet. Quarter past two is engraved on my mind in letters of fire!'

'It's two prompt, Jossy!'

'Two it is. Just joking, pet.' He turned to the lads again. 'Ross! Stir yourself. You're standing there like one o'clock half struck.' To Glenda he said, 'Look, precious, the wedding's all sewn up – but the lads have got to train.'

Glenda seemed put out as Jossy looked alternately at her and at the lads. But she was not one to stay quiet very long when she had points to make.

'You have booked suits for Albert, Bob and yourself, Jossy?'

Certain that the lads were giving one hundred per cent effort to the training, Jossy gave Glenda his full attention. 'Look, pet, me and Albert will look so smart in them monkey suits that we'll probably be signed up as male models. We'll be doing pullovers and scarves for Bilberry and Jagger in the Sunday Times colour bit soon.'

The new mood pleased Glenda. 'And you promise me you won't wear your white socks,' she twinkled.

'Scout's honour!' Jossy pecked her on the cheek. Glenda went off happy and Jossy turned back to Albert,

119

who was chatting to Wayne as the lads began larking about. Glenn, Selly and Ross were Cossack dancing on their haunches.

'When it comes to discipline,' Jossy shrieked, 'you're about as firm as a muesli bar, Albert.'

Albert had been earwigging on Jossy's conversation with Glenda. 'At least when I make arrangements with people they are fair, square and above board.'

Jossy looked hard at him and Albert looked hard back. Jossy wilted.

'I'm trying to balance what I owe Glenda with what I owe the team,' bleated Jossy.

The boys saved Jossy from further criticism from Albert. Ricky stepped forward, his tousled hair wet with sweat. He gripped Jossy, man-to-man, by the arm. 'There's really no need for you to attend the match on Saturday, Boss. We'll do the business, won't we fellas?'

'Yeah,' Ross agreed. 'Take it easy. Have a bath, cover yourself in talc.'

Jossy was stunned. 'Look lads, this is the Cup. I have to be at that match.'

'You're daft, Boss,' Wayne grinned. 'Just concentrate on your wedding and we'll see you at the reception – glorious and victorious.' The rest of the lads growled their agreement.

Jossy was by now fairly narked. 'Will you lot forget about my wedding . . .'

Albert chipped in. 'The lads do have a point. Saturday's a big day for other people!'

'You don't have to lecture me on my duties, Albert Hanson.' Jossy began speaking like a general on the eve of a particularly bloody battle. 'Saturday will be a day for split-second timing. I don't want any broken hopes or broken hearts.'

Albert raised his eyes for divine guidance as Jossy

chuntered on. 'I know that Sharkey's Express will come at us like tigers, bright of eye, sharp of tooth . . .'

The lads and Albert were spared any more of this hot air by the appearance of Bob. And what an appearance it was. When Bob got a new obsession, he indulged it in style. This week he had decided to show Steven Spielberg and the lads what movie making was all about. He was toting enough equipment to broadcast a royal wedding: video camera, mikes on wires that stuck out like spikes on a hedgehog, even a battery-operated clapperboard. His eyes were glued to his camera as he photographed the lads.

'Keep it natural, chaps. Don't play to the camera.' Bob nosed amongst them like a bear after food. Jossy was not amused. Bob clapped the board in front of Jossy's nose and identified his shot. 'Take 1. Manager Blair. Sync chat. Talk now, Jossy.' Bob dived forward, camera menacing.

'Bob, you're getting in the way of an essential practice session.' Jossy spoke through gritted teeth.

Bob raised himself to his full height. He assumed the expression of an enthusiast shamefully slammed down. 'I know the importance of this practice session and of Saturday's match. That is why I am helping!'

More than one eyebrow was raised in amazement.

'Helping? You've lost me, old son,' said Albert.

Bob went on after an extremely theatrical pause. 'I am making a training film. My video camera will record every move in your training. Then coach Blair can sit back and replay it all. He can analyse strengths and weaknesses.'

The mockery disappeared like dew before sunlight. Bob wallowed in the warm glances, even from his son Ross.

'It's great gear, Bob. Must have cost you a fortune.' Jossy was very impressed.

Bob became modest. 'I've got contacts, son. I keep them happy, they keep me happy.' Bob leaned forward and smarmed to Jossy. 'I was planning to do a real "Close Encounters" job on your wedding, sunshine. Close-ups! Moody dissolves! A bit of Doris Day haze around the blushing bride . . .'

Albert's rasping tone re-arranged Jossy's approving grin. 'Here, Jossy. Does the blushing bride know about this cup match at eleven on Saturday, or does she not?'

There was a silence as Jossy took Albert by the collar of his tracksuit. 'No, comrade, Glenda does not know. And she's not going to find out, is she?'

The boys glowered at Albert. He shut up, but he was thinking the very worst.

A couple of days later, Glenda's bedroom was the scene of hectic activity. Glenda was sitting down with a needle and thread, making alterations to a bridesmaid's dress, while Opal and Shaz busied themselves decorating the head-dresses. Melanie had her dress on and was twirling merrily in front of a full-length mirror. The wedding had sparked off all kinds of hopes and fantasies in the girls.

Shaz admired Glenda's dress. 'I'm going to have one like this when I marry Ricky.' Shaz shook her long brown hair and stroked her thin nose thoughtfully. 'And he'll be in a charcoal grey coat, with striped trousers and he'll have a cravat and a pearl pin.'

'And the arrangements, I'm sure, will be computerized. Punch cards instead of invitations.' Glenda's amusement was affectionate.

Opal looked her usual puzzled self. 'If Harvey and me got married I want something very quiet . . .'

'. . . and you'll want a fur coat, love. It'll be chilly getting married down at the ice rink.' Glenda's good humour knew no bounds.

'Glenn and Selly would probably want to get married in a disco,' trilled Melanie.

'With everybody in spiked hairdos and swinging chains instead of holding bouquets!' Shaz's comment set them all off giggling.

'What's Jossy going to be wearing, Glenda? Not a black-and-white striped cravat, I hope!' Opal's joke hit a nerve in Glenda. She stopped sewing and a frigid note came into her voice.

'Oh, no, love. On my wedding day football will be firmly in second place. Jossy has been measured up for top hat, tailcoat and waistcoat, all in the most restrained silver grey . . .'

Tracey came in and immediately sensed the coolness in Glenda's mood. 'I hope everything goes according to plan on Saturday, Glenda,' Tracey smiled confidently.

Glenda forced a wide grin. 'What could possibly go wrong my dear?' She held up the dress she had been working on. 'Now try this on.'

Tracey took the dress and began changing. She spoke to fill the silence.

'Have you thought about all the jobs you'll have to do for the Giants when you're married, Glenda?' Tracey's words brought back the smiles all round.

'Painting the touchlines,' said Opal.

'Polishing the trophies,' said Shaz.

'Calming Jossy down when the lads lose,' giggled Melanie.

'By seven flukey goals, of course,' added Tracey, as she fastened the last button of her dress.

'You look lovely, dear,' Glenda smiled. Then the ice returned to her voice. 'No football match, be it in a back street or at Wembley stadium, is going to cast a shadow over my – I mean our – big day!'

The girls nodded. Only Tracey's eyes held the slightest doubt.

Later the same evening nostalgia was flowing like Sloane's liniment at Magpie Sports. It was Jossy's Stag Night and a rare feast had been consumed. There had been pease pudding and ham sandwiches and Geordie leek broth. Now the lads were into parkin pigs and cans of fizz.

Jossy and Albert sat in the middle of this, supping cans of bitter. Bob hustled around adjusting his moveable lights before aiming his video camera. In the middle of the shop, one of the dummies was wearing Jossy's wedding outfit. It stood like a totem pole, symbol of a new religion – marriage and all that went with it.

'I can't wait to see you at the wedding, Jossy. Your finest hour.' Albert was almost on the verge of tears.

Jossy was on him like a teacher on a dunce. 'Hang on, Albert. Surely my – our – finest hour was when we beat the Dets in the Cup Final. Remember my late pep talk, Rick?'

Ricky's eyes glowed. 'Yes, it was great. It really turned the tide. Even if the ref did chew my ears off.'

'We've had some great times since I dragged you lot out of the gutter,' said Jossy.

The lads all nodded. Bob was fluttering about with his camera.

'Hey, Jossy. Let's have a shot of you by the dummy.'

'Why by the dummy?' Jossy was still able to find possible insult even in a party atmosphere.

'No offence, Jossy,' muttered Bob. 'It's just the mood I want to capture. Silly yet deep at the same time.'

'The story of our lives,' wailed Albert under his breath. He raised his voice. 'Calm down, Jossy, you're as touchy as a tick. Marriage is not the end of the world.'

Jossy looked wistful. 'But I've had the best years of my life as a bachelor, Albert. The football, the friendship, the fun . . .'

The boys crowded round. Harvey had his serious look on.

'I want to know if you're planning to have a big family, Boss.' The idea caught fire in Harvey's brain. 'I know. You can name the kids after us. Harvey Blair, Ricky Blair . . .'

'Yogi Blair,' laughed Glenn.

Ross pushed his way through the throng and, slightly embarrassed, offered Jossy an untidily wrapped parcel.

'Me and the lads clubbed together to buy you these for your new life.'

Jossy tore off the paper and held up a pair of suede carpet slippers with a fleecy lining. His face curled into a mask.

'Slippers! Carpet slippers. What a cheek! You'd think I had one foot in the grave.' He began chasing Ross round the shop, taking swipes at his head with the slippers.

'They'll be good for sitting by the fire, Boss,' said Glenn.

'They'll go well with your rocking-chair!' cried Selly.

Bob had packed in his shooting. Now he took centre stage and pulled out a thick book of jokes. There were loud groans.

'Let's have a bit of respect for the best man.' Bob cleared his throat. 'Now, after the hurly-burly of the wedding, I will lighten the proceedings at the reception.'

'Do you have to, Dad?' Ross's voice was plaintive. 'At the last bookies' dinner you got the slow handclap.'

Bob sniffed loudly and delved into the book. Harvey had him weighed up.

'I'll bet he goes straight for the mother-in-law routines.'

Bob's eyes gleamed. 'I say, I say. I've got my mother-in-law a summer job. Can you guess where?'

'Easy,' said Ricky dryly. 'Swimming around in Loch Ness.'

'You've been clocking my book,' said Bob, hurt.

'Any jokes in there about lady councillors?' asked Glenn cheekily.

'Just you watch it, smarty,' said Jossy, wagging his finger.

The evening continued with yarns about the great victories of the past and, as it drew to a close, Jossy had almost forgotten about his wedding. Bob and Albert brought him back down to earth.

'On Saturday I shall call to collect the bride at 1.30 p.m. prompt.' Albert's eyes glowed and he stood erect as if he was back in the army. 'At precisely 2 p.m. I shall be at the altar of Glipton St Michael's with the bride . . .'

'Roger. And over to me,' rapped Bob. 'The match starts at 11 a.m. prompt and the final whistle is at 12.45. So – I shall be escorting the groom here away from St James's Park at one o'clock on the dot. It's a cinch!'

'It sure is. The Express aren't playing badly but I reckon we've got the edge.' Jossy was still in the clouds.

'You are getting married on Saturday, Jossy,' emphasised Albert.

'I know, I know,' said Jossy tetchily.

'Three cheers for Jossy and Glenda!' cried Ricky. The lads bellowed them out as Jossy looked embarrassed. But deep inside he felt good.

THIRTEEN

The Saturday of the wedding dawned bright but with a hint of mist hanging in the damp autumn air over St James's Park. Jossy and Albert arrived at the ground via Albert's motorbike and sidecar at ten o'clock. While Albert brewed up, Jossy went for a walk around the pitch. He stopped by the giant oak tree on the far side from the stand and looked round, remembering the bunch of scruffs he had come across when they were the Glipton Grasshoppers. Glenn and Selly colliding in midfield; Harvey looking like an agitated stick insect in goal; Albert tearing his hair out in despair.

Tracey broke the reverie. She came up quietly behind him, carrying his and Albert's morning suits in plastic covers. 'Remembering the good times, Jossy?' Her voice was soft.

'Aye, lassie. We've had some of them, haven't we, thanks to you and your brains. You got us out of some scrapes.'

'Well, you've got Glenda's brains to help as well now. Marriage will do you good.' Tracey talked as if she was sixty and a grandmother.

'Come on,' said Jossy, 'let's have a cuppa before the fun starts.'

The fun started half an hour later when Jossy walked out of the changing rooms and saw Bob's latest bit of directorial equipment. Behind one of the goals, a couple of Bob's men were erecting a ten-foot-high platform. Jossy and Albert dashed over.

'What's this, Bob? Not another advertising deal?' asked Jossy.

'No, Jossy.' Bob was glowing with pride. 'That's my perch. I'll be up there during the game shooting away. We call it a top shot. You'll be able to see the angle of every pass when I play it back to you.'

Jossy nodded. He turned to Albert. 'Next thing you know he'll have a collapsible chair with his name on the back.'

Bob winked at Albert. Albert hated to think what it might mean.

Jossy hustled into the dressing-room where the lads were nearly ready to take the field. Ricky was looking at his watch. 'I don't like the look of this, Boss. It's fifteen minutes to kick-off and there's no sign of Sharkey and the Express lads.' Ricky's freckled face showed concern. 'We don't want no delays today, do we?'

Jossy shook his head. He cast a glance at the two Moss Bros. suits that Tracey had hung up carefully. 'No, we don't, kidda. And it's not like Sharkey to be late for any game.'

He called the lads round for some last-minute advice. There was a noise of footsteps in the corridor and Albert ran in.

'Dave Sharkey in a phone-box ringing you, Jossy. It sounds like trouble.'

'He picks his days to have bother,' said Jossy, almost desperately, as he ran out to take the call.

Squeaky noises were coming out of the receiver that Albert had left lying on the rack.

'He'll blow a fuse in a minute,' said Ross, who had led a small posse of the lads out behind Jossy.

Jossy picked up the phone and listened to Dave's rantings for a few seconds. 'Let's get this straight,

128

Dave.' Jossy had on his pompous hat. He was playing to the lads. 'I was under the impression that a match of cup football was due to be commencing here at St James's Park in a matter of minutes.'

The voice on the other end of the phone grew loud enough for the lads to hear. Jossy held the receiver a good six inches from his ear. Sharkey's voice almost spat the words out. 'If you will stop taking the rise for a minute, Blair, I will convey certain information apropos a malfunction in our transport arrangements.'

Jossy grinned. 'In plain English, you mean that your bus has conked out?' The lads laughed.

Sharkey's words came out like needles. 'The vehicle has, as you suggest, a temporary fault. It's no fault of mine.'

'Now, Dave, I know you.' Jossy was still being impish. 'This is not some smart psychological ploy to put my lads off is it?'

'I would not stoop to anything so low,' came the clipped, almost hurt, answer.

'Dave, you would limbo dance underneath a swing door if you thought it would get you the drop on the opposition,' chirruped Jossy.

A burst of the old Dave Sharkey came over. 'We will be at St James's Park, Blair, if we have to crawl – and we will run you ragged.'

Jossy looked at his watch and the grin left his face. He was beginning to see all sorts of pitfalls. 'Now look here, Dave, I think we should both simmer down.' Jossy was now grovelling. 'You do realize that I have more than one important fixture on my hands today?'

Sharkey's voice rang out triumphant. 'Exactly, Jossy Blair. So if you would listen, we might both get nearer fulfilling our mutual obligations. If this bus does not get going in fifteen minutes, we will proceed by taxi.'

Jossy panicked and then began pleading. 'Shout

Shazam and come in a puff of smoke, Dave, but get here!'

The phone at the other end went down with a bang.

Tracey was looking worried. 'The Express won't be here much before half past eleven,' she frowned. 'That's going to make things very tight.'

'I know, woman,' shouted Jossy. 'But if there's no more hiccups I should have half an hour between the final whistle and the wedding.'

Bob bundled into the dressing-room, carrying a piece of canvas and metal.

'Can anybody put one of these up?' He held up a collapsible chair pathetically.

Tracey grabbed it from him. She flicked it and it went up. It had *Robert Nelson – DIRECTOR* in big letters on the back. 'Here's the wedding day falling about our ears and all the best man's bothered about is his fancy chair.' Tracey banged the chair on the floor and it collapsed.

It was Jossy's theory that sometimes movement was a sound substitute for action. 'Tracey, let's get this show on the road. You and Albert shoot off to Glenda's. Pretend everything's fine. Don't say there's a football match on.'

Albert grabbed his monkey suit and Tracey made for the door.

'Tracey.' Jossy was on the rack. 'Give her one hundred per cent man-made fibre, high quality flannel. Put the clocks back. Anything. But don't let her twig that there are any problems.'

Bob stepped in. 'Take the keys to my Merc, Albert. It'll get you there faster.' He turned to Jossy. 'And if I were you I'd get into my glad rags. Just in case.'

Jossy began stripping off his tracksuit.

130

Glenda Fletcher was certainly looking her very best. Her long brown hair had been teased out to show its natural waves and her complexion was glowing enough to need just a dab of make-up. She had visions of Jossy lounging in a foam bath singing 'Blaydon Races'. He's a bit of a laddo at times, but he's canny, thought Glenda. She had just the slightest flutterings of butter-flies in her tummy. But, as a veteran of some very heavy council meetings, she knew how to control her nerves.

'Jossy's probably just getting out of the bath and starting to dress,' said Glenda to her three bridesmaids. 'I wonder where Tracey is? It's not like her to be late.'

Opal, Shaz and Melanie looked at each other. They all knew about the cup match. To avoid the flak, they began admiring Glenda's wedding dress.

'It's lovely material,' said Opal.

'I might be a bit more trendy,' said Melanie.

'Leopardskin?' asked Shaz sarcastically.

Melanie gave her a friendly punch.

The girls nearly gasped with relief when Tracey tiptoed into the room. Glenda was still fixated on the mirror. Shushing the girls, Tracey went straight to the clock on the dresser that was showing the time as twelve o'clock. Tracey wound it back fifteen minutes. She winked at Opal.

Opal twigged. 'Well, we've got plenty of time. It's not twelve yet.'

Glenda toddled over the room and looked at the clock. She turned to Tracey. 'I can't wait to see you properly done up as a bridesmaid. Get changed, dear.'

There was a polite coughing from outside the door.

'Is that you, Albert? My, you are early. Have you brought the bouquets?' asked Glenda.

'Do I have the blushing bride's permission to enter her boudoir?' Albert was laying it on thick.

'Entrez,' trilled Glenda.

Albert slithered in, blushing, the bridesmaid's bouquets held forward.

Glenda frowned at him. Albert cringed, thinking that somehow she was suspicious. 'Isn't it time you were in the proper attire, Albert? You are giving me away, aren't you?'

'Plenty of time, love. Plenty.' Albert winked at Tracey. She mouthed the word 'flannel' to him.

'Well,' stammered Albert. 'Things are going so well, I reckon we should all put our feet up and have a nice cuppa.'

Glenda started to protest. Tracey stepped in. 'Albert's right. Those wedding bells will sound all the sweeter after elevenses.'

Glenda sat down. 'I do hope that Jossy's suit fits.'

Albert spoke soft and warm. 'He won't let you down, love. I've never seen him take such pains with his appearance. He's as dapper as a king penguin.'

In fact, Jossy looked more like a hungry vulture. The Express and Sharkey had arrived and the lads were getting changed, but the monkey suit was taking some getting on. Bob was helping with the trousers as Jossy fought the cravat.

'Stand still, Jossy.' Bob tugged at the braces. 'This isn't a parachute harness.'

'I'll be for the high jump if Glenda finds out about the match.' Jossy had the stiff collar front round near his ear.

'Look, pal,' said Bob, man-to-man, 'she's going to find out some time. Break it to her gently over a good bottle of wine and a candle-lit dinner in old Sorrento.'

At last Jossy bore some resemblance to the newspaper adverts of an up-market bridegroom.

'You have got the plane tickets and all the hotel bumf, haven't you, Bob?'

'Don't worry. Stay cool.' Bob placed the topper on Jossy's head and stifled a giggle.

'What's up, Bob?'

'Nothing.' Bob tried to muffle his mirth. 'But I've never seen you dressed up before.'

There was a clatter of studs and Ricky stuck his head round the door.

'Get your skates on, Boss. It's nearly twelve. Sharkey's chewing the grass and the ref's doing a James Galway on the whistle.

'OK, Rick. Give them what for!' Jossy adjusted the topper to a jaunty angle. 'And if Dave Sharkey says one word about me prowling the touchline in a monkey suit, I'll plant him one.'

Bob ushered Jossy out of the door. The two parted company as they neared the pitch. Bob, with his collapsible chair, light meter and video gear, climbed his tower behind the goal. The Express keeper looked up at him.

'You're at the wrong end for the action, pal,' said the goalie.

'We'll see about that, pal,' snapped Bob.

Ignoring one or two smirks and puzzled looks, Jossy strode along the touchline to where Sharkey was poised in his usual hawkish stance. He gave Jossy a sideways look, but the gleam in his eyes showed no amusement.

'I hope you get what you deserve today, Blair.'

Jossy sensed the double meaning. He had, in fact, invited Sharkey to the wedding reception that evening.

'One thing at a time, Dave,' purred Jossy.

133

FOURTEEN

'Howway, the lads!' Jossy cheered his lads on as the whistle shrilled and Ross got the game going. The Giants were on the attack and the Express centre half cleared the ball halfway to the canal.

'Method, Express,' screamed Sharkey. 'Maintain method.'

'Singe them, Ross. That's my boy!' Jossy had his topper off and was waving it as Ross cut in from the wing at top speed. The Express fell back, expecting a cross. Ross walloped the ball over the defence and the centre half jumped. He missed. The goalie was unsighted as the ball curved past his right arm and into the net. The lads mobbed Ross.

'What a fluke! It was a cross!' yelled Sharkey.

'No,' laughed Jossy. 'It was a shot. A banana shot.'

On the tower behind the Express goal, Bob was going spare.

'There's a long way to go yet, Jossy.' Sharkey had regained his composure.

'You don't have to remind me, Dave.' Jossy's jubilation evaporated. 'I only hope my flannel squad is doing the business,' he said, under his breath.

Albert was in the hall of Glenda's house, since all the other rooms were full of women. He had changed into his monkey suit and was now viewing the result in the

134

mirror. 'I'm smarter than I was at my own wedding,' he muttered to himself.

Glenda's dulcet tones echoed down the stairs. 'I can't wait to see you, Albert. All done up like a dog's dinner.'

Albert winced. 'She'll make me look like a dog's breakfast if she cottons on about the match.' He raised his voice. 'I'm ready and we've bags of time. I'll just check to see if your carriage and four is here.'

A shadow loomed through the frosted glass of Glenda's front door. A hand raised to knock. Albert had the letter box open in a flash.

'Here, sunshine, drive slowly round the block a few times, will you? We've got a bit of pre-match nerves in here.'

'Right, chief,' said the driver and went off.

Albert stood upright, tugged at the stiff collar that was throttling him and shouted. 'There's no sign of the jam jar and chauffeur yet, Glenda. He must be giving it a right good clean and polish.'

'Fine, simply fine, Albert.' Glenda began to sing in Italian.

Tracey tripped downstairs looking radiant in her bridesmaid's dress. She frowned. 'We can't keep this con job up much longer, Albert. She's like a whippet on a leash up there. And she's not daft.'

'You're right,' said Albert. 'It's a quarter to one now. I wonder how things are going at the match.'

The half-time interval was drawing to a close and the Giants were still winning one–nil. Jossy knelt in a huddle, pepping up the lads. He had dished out the half-time oranges and quite a lot of the juice had spilt down his pearl-grey waistcoat.

'So my last words to you are – hang in there. You're playing great.'

135

Jossy was fed up with Sharkey's patter, so he took up a position beneath Bob's tower. In front of him Harvey paced the goalmouth like a tiger.

'Make that ball yours if it comes near,' Jossy growled to Harvey.

After a hectic half hour the score was still one–nil, but the Express were putting on the pressure. Sharkey shuffled up to Jossy and began the tirade.

'Eliminate error, Express,' Sharkey spouted. 'Be spacially aware.'

Jossy howled with laughter. 'I've heard it all now. You make those words up, don't you, Dave?'

Sharkey did not deign to give Jossy an answer. But a minute later he really did hit a nerve. He saw that Jossy was anxiously looking at his watch. Sharkey's dark eyebrows almost joined up. He leered.

'Your mind's not on this match, Jossy. You're miles away. You should have got on with your wedding and left Albert in charge!'

Sharkey had lit Jossy's blue touch paper. He took off the topper and crashed it on to the grass.

'That is a gross insult, Dave Sharkey. I am not – repeat not – thinking about any rotten wedding!' Jossy was almost dancing with rage.

Smiling like Christopher Lee spotting a blood bank, Sharkey reached down and lifted up the topper. It was now streaked with mud. He replaced it on Jossy's head.

'My, who's a pretty boy, then.'

Albert and Tracey's delaying tactics were still working well at twenty-five minutes to two. The cars pulled up outside Glenda's house and the entourage got under way: Glenda and Albert were in the first car and the bridesmaids were in the second. Glenda was too excited to talk as they neared St Michael's Church.

But when the car stopped at the church, Albert got

a shock. There were still people outside and there was no sign of Bob, Jossy or any of the lads. They stood aside as Glenda looked round then trotted into the church. She was out in a matter of seconds and her face was like thunder.

'A great pair of friends you two turned out to be. Right! Out with it. Jossy Blair is not in that church. Where is he?'

Albert looked to heaven. 'He's at St James's Park . . .'

'At a cup match,' added Tracey. 'They must be playing extra time.'

'I'll give him extra time – in a salt mine!' Glenda was purple with rage. 'Where have the cars gone?'

Albert looked round. 'For a cuppa, I suppose. The drivers usually do.'

'Right. Follow me!' Glenda stormed off down the street and the puzzled entourage followed. She was not long in taking decisive action. An ambulance came cruising by and Glenda flagged it down with her bouquet. She jumped in the front with Albert and ordered the driver to let the bridesmaids into the back. He did as he was told.

The driver put his foot down and got to the business. 'Where's the accident, Missus?'

'Miss!' said Glenda, pointedly. 'The accident has not actually happened yet.' Her tone was ice cold. 'But it will occur at St James's Park football ground in exactly five minutes' time. It will affect a white Caucasian person, male, about 37 years of age and of less than average intelligence.'

The driver was wide-eyed. 'Type of injury?'

'Oh, I don't know,' mused Glenda. 'Grievous bodily harm to the earhole, I think, for starters. Then a quick forearm smash. What do you reckon, Albert?'

'No more than he deserves,' mumbled Albert.

A big grin spread across the driver's face. 'This job's looking up all of a sudden. We don't usually arrive before the accident.'

At St James's Park it was all happening. The score was still one–nil. On the tower behind Harvey's goal, Bob was going spare. He held his camera in one hand and waved the other as the Express mounted an attack.

'Get behind the ball, Giants,' Bob screamed. 'Only two minutes to go. They shall not pass.'

In his excitement, Bob dropped the camera and it fell with a thud behind Harvey. Harvey turned to look and the Express centre forward shot. Harvey turned back too late. It was one–one. Jossy was up the ladder to Bob in a flash. He shook him by the collar of his overalls.

'That was sabotage!' Jossy fumed. 'I ought to wrap this gear round your lugs.'

Sharkey looked up at the two of them. 'Yet another Giants' diversion, is it? Catchweight contest?' He looked at his watch. 'We'll probably have to go into extra time.'

Jossy and Bob stopped tussling. Both looked worried sick. As Jossy descended the ladder, the whistle went for full time. Sharkey was waiting for him and together they strode across the turf to address their flopped-out troops. The Giants shook their heads sadly. Ricky stopped massaging his legs and looked up. 'Sorry we couldn't get a result in proper time, Boss.'

'Never mind, lads. I'm sure you'll do me proud in extra time.' Jossy looked at his watch which was now reading ten minutes to two.

Sharkey came over with the ref. He winked at Jossy. 'I've suggested five minutes each way to settle it. Might help your other – er – match.'

The ref nodded and Jossy felt like hugging Sharkey. 'Thanks, Dave.'

Jossy was covered in mud from head to toe. He started to brush himself down but only made matters worse. He looked as though he had been sleeping the night in a ploughed field. Looking earnestly at the lads, he said pleadingly, 'Look, fellas, I'll have to go to the church now and leave you to it. Glenda's going to be on the warpath as it is, so . . .'

He saw their heads fall. He reasoned with them. 'Lads, it's my wedding day! Give us a break. She'll boil me in oil.'

'I'm shaking like a leaf, Boss. You've got to stay.' Ross's voice was trembling.

'He's right, Boss, we all need you,' said Ricky.

'You've burnt your boats, Boss. What difference will another ten minutes make?' Harvey's point swung the argument.

'OK lads. I'll stay.' Jossy looked like a man waiting for the firing squad. 'But don't let me down.'

As the lads rushed to re-start play, Jossy looked round for moral support from Bob but he was nowhere to be seen. He took up his lonely vigil on the touchline.

The first nine minutes of extra time were as exciting as any the Glipton Giants had ever taken part in. It was end to end stuff with players dropping with cramp at regular intervals. Jossy was hoarse and too worried to say much anyway. But he started to jump as Glenn walked his way through midfield. Ricky started a forward run and Ross began yelling for the ball from the right wing. Jossy noticed that the Express central defenders were dragging their legs.

'Early ball, down the middle!' yelled Jossy.

Glenn whacked the ball high into the area. Ricky poised for a header, only to be flattened by the Express keeper.

'Penalty!' screamed Jossy and the lads.

The referee pointed to the spot. Jossy waited confidently for Ricky to take the kick and win the match. But Ricky was hanging back.

'Go on, Rick. Bury it!' shouted Jossy.

'I can't, Boss. Me shot's too weak. Ross, you take it!' Ricky was adamant.

'No. I'm scared,' said Ross.

Jossy's fury increased as everyone except Harvey and little Daz chickened out.

'Daz! You take it!' he yelled.

Daz frowned with concentration and pushed his curls of dark hair out of his eyes. He placed the ball carefully on the spot and wiped the toe of his right boot.

'Come on, my son, show these big guys how to go on,' shouted Jossy.

Daz paced out six steps, gave a thumbs up to Jossy and pasted the ball as hard as he could. The ball flew hard, straight at the Express goalie who had committed himself to a dive to the right. The ball zipped along the ground and into the net.

'Goal!' screamed Jossy, as the lads mobbed Daz.

The ambulance siren could just be heard above the cheers. Jossy looked up and saw the bridesmaids coming out of the back doors.

'My word, the mountain has come to Mohammed,' said Sharkey, seeing Glenda's scowling face in the cab next to the driver. She leapt from the ambulance and approached Jossy like a white tornado.

Just then the final whistle blew. The Giants were the cup winners.

Glenda reached Jossy as the lads surrounded him trying to scrape the mud from his monkey suit.

'I know I've cut it a bit fine, pet, but I can explain everything,' wailed Jossy.

'I'd like to cut you fine, Jossy Blair, stick you on a skewer and serve you up as a kebab. It should have been our proudest day and here's you in the middle of a field looking like Worzel Gummidge.' Glenda was waving her bouquet about like an Amazon with a new axe.

'He looked real super-dudey at the kick off, Glenda, honest,' offered Harvey.

A new noise echoed over St James's Park; the harsh squawking of the old horn on Albert's motorbike and sidecar. Everyone looked round to see Bob on the bike and the Reverend Timothy Barnflower in the sidecar.

'I don't believe it,' sighed Sharkey.

Bob ran up beaming. He tore off his overalls to reveal an immaculate morning suit. He pulled out a letter.

'I have known Joswell Blair for a long time and . . . as insurance, I wrote to the Archbishop of Canterbury . . .'

'A personal friend, no doubt,' hissed Harvey.

'. . . asking him for a special dispensation to have the wedding here at St James's Park if necessary. So – let's have the very best of order please!'

FIFTEEN

The wedding reception at Glipton Community Centre was coming to a close. Glenda and Jossy sat smiling in pride of place as Bob finished his jokes and toasts.

'Finally, ladies and gentlemen, boys and girls, honoured guests – including Dave Sharkey – pray silence for a man who has had an extremely harrowing day – the bridegroom, Joswell Blair.'

There was loud applause as Jossy stood up. He tried to look serious, as befitted the occasion, but he was having trouble. Most of the lads were pulling faces and trying to make him laugh.

'Lads and lasses. One way and another it's been a right canny day.' Jossy looked round the room. 'It's been a day of triumph and near misses . . .' Glenda led the applause for this. 'It's been the kind of day that calls for humility – and, as you know, there's nobody more humile than me.' Wayne led a few gentle jeers. 'Straight up, though, I'm thrilled to skinny ribbons that Glenda has chosen me to be her fella. I reckon we'll make a good team. I'm sorry that these proceedings have run to extra time.'

There was laughter and loud applause. Glenda stood up and some of the Giants cowered, thinking that a tongue lashing was on the cards.

'Thank you all for attending a great day for myself and Jossy.' She raised her glass. The lads were still expecting at least a nasty dig. 'I'd like to salute the

Glipton Giants for a great achievement in the cup match today. Beating the Express two–one was a wonderful result.'

A great roar exploded round the hall. Toasts were drunk and Sharkey spluttered with fury. Albert stood up with a grin on his face.

'Now, ladies and gentlemen, we'd like to bring the proceedings to a close with a special treat. As most of you will know, our own club benefactor, Bob Nelson – Glipton's answer to Otto Preminger – has been working on a video for weeks now.' Bob glowed with pride. 'So I'd like you all to sit back and enjoy its world première. You haven't much option since Bob has locked all the doors and put glue on the seats!'

There was generous applause as Bob took his place by the video machine.

'I have very rapidly put a commentary on my work . . .' He said 'work' with hushed reverence. Harvey giggled. Ross blushed. 'I see the film as a piece of *ciné veritée* . . .'

'Cine very tatty,' quipped Albert.

'Come on, Bob, fast forward yourself,' shouted Wayne.

Unruffled, Bob went on, 'I proudly present – Giant Jamboree – un film de Robert Nelson!'

The lights went down to a chorus of boos and whistles. Up came the first pictures on the screen, backs of boys' heads, so out of focus that the lads could not identify themselves. Bob's recorded voice rang out, 'Glipton Giants are based at beautiful St James's Park . . .' The picture changed to cockeyed shots of Tracey and the rest of the bridesmaids. Bob's voice droned on, 'The team are a stout bunch of lads, fit for anything . . .'

The laughter increased as Bob's commentary became more and more out of sync with the pictures.

Even Sharkey had tears of mirth in his eyes. Despite the hilarity all around him, Bob sat with a benign smile on his face.

Jossy and Glenda slipped out quietly.

A couple of hours later Bob and Albert were having a pint in The British Connection.

'Did you mean to make your film a comedy?' asked Albert innocently.

'No. But once I dropped the camera at the match, everything went on the blink. Still, it went down well, didn't it?' Bob needed the praise.

'Ace,' said Albert. He looked at his watch. 'Half past eight. Do you think he'll be telling her the news?'

'What news?' asked Bob.

Glenda and Jossy had been sitting in the car travelling north on the A1 for well over an hour. Now the first pit heaps round Chester-le-Street could be seen by the roadside. She turned to Jossy, whose eyes were intent on the road.

'Did we really have to fly from *Newcastle* to Sorrento, Jossy? Surely Manchester would have been more convenient?'

'Oh, well, we're not going tonight, pet.' Jossy kept on looking straight ahead. 'I thought we'd stay in Newcastle tonight. Then we can go and watch the lads play Inter Milan in a friendly at St James's tomorrow, and then it's perfect for getting the six o'clock plane to Rome and on to Sorrento. It's a doddle!'

'You what, Jossy Blair?' said Glenda, 'I'm going to strangle you!!'

If Walls Could Talk

Lucy Worsley is a leading young historian. In addition to her day job as Chief Curator at Historic Royal Palaces, she appears regularly on radio and television. Lucy is the author of *Cavalier: A Tale of Chivalry, Passion and Great Houses* (2007) and *Courtiers: The Secret History of Kensington Palace* (2010).

Praise for *If Walls Could Talk*:
'I can think of no finer guide than Lucy Worsley to the long and curious history of the home.' Simon Jenkins

'Saucy intimacies and salacious secrets . . . I was glued.' *Country Life*

Praise for Lucy Worsley:
'An immensely talented and innovative historian.' *Mail on Sunday*

'Worsley is a gifted storyteller, as deft at tracing developments as she is in homing in on amusing detail.' *Sunday Times*

'Worsley's style is wonderfully readable and her talent for empathy enormous.' *Sunday Telegraph*

'Worsley is like the enthusiastic history teacher you never had, who wants to make learning as fun as possible.' *Guardian*

'The impression Worsley gives is that she lives and breathes English history.' *Evening Standard*

'The kind of captivating history I most enjoy.' Antonia Fraser

'Worsley has shown herself to be an engaging, sometimes unconventional guide to the habits and customs of bygone Britons.' *Boston Globe*

by the same author

CAVALIER: A TALE OF CHIVALRY, PASSION AND GREAT HOUSES
COURTIERS: THE SECRET HISTORY OF THE GEORGIAN COURT